MARRIAGE:
TO CLAIM
HIS TWINS

MARRIAGE: TO CLAIM HIS TWINS

BY

PENNY JORDAN

MILLS & BOON®

First published in Great Britain 2010
Large Print edition 2010
Harlequin Mills & Boon Limited,
Eton House, 18-24 Paradise Road,
Richmond, Surrey TW9 1SR

© Penny Jordan 2010

ISBN: 978 0 263 21244 0

Harlequin Mills & Boon policy is to use papers that are
natural, renewable and recyclable products and made
from wood grown in sustainable forests. The logging and
manufacturing process conform to the legal environmental
regulations of the country of origin.

Printed and bound in Great Britain
by CPI Antony Rowe, Chippenham, Wiltshire

PROLOGUE

ALEXANDER KONSTANTINAKOS, powerful, formidable, billionaire head of an internationally renowned container shipping line originally founded by his late grandfather, stood in the middle of the elegantly luxurious drawing room of his home on the Greek Ionian island of Theopolis, his gaze riveted on the faces of the twin boys in the photograph he was holding.

Two black-haired, olive-skinned and dark-eyed identical faces looked back at him, their mother kneeling down beside them. The three of them were shabbily dressed in cheap-looking clothes.

Tall, dark-haired, with the features of two thousand years of alpha-male warriors and victors sculpted into the bones of his handsome face the same way that their determination was sculpted into his psyche, he stood in the now silent room, the accusation his sister had just made was still echoing through his head.

'They have to be your sons,' she had accused Nikos, their younger brother. 'They have our family features stamped on them, and you were at university in Manchester.'

Alexander—Sander to his family—didn't need to keep gazing at the photograph Elena had taken with her mobile phone on her way through Manchester Airport after visiting her husband's family to confirm her statement, or to memorise the boys' faces. They were already carved into his memory for all time.

'I don't know anything about them,' his younger brother Nikos denied, breaking the silence. 'They aren't mine, Sander, I promise you. Please believe me.'

'Of course they're yours,' Elena corrected their younger brother. 'Just look at those faces.

Nikos is lying, Sander. Those children are of our blood.'

Sander looked at his younger sister and brother, on the verge of quarrelling just as they had always done as children. There were only two years between them, but he had been born five years before Elena and seven before Nikos, and after their grandfather's death as the only adult family member left in their lives he had naturally taken on the responsibility of acting as a father figure to them. That had often meant arbitrating between them when they argued.

This time, though, it wasn't arbitration that was called for.

Sander looked at the photograph again and then announced curtly, 'Of our blood, but not of Nikos's making. Nikos is speaking the truth. The children are not his.'

Elena stared at him.

'How can you know that?'

Sander turned towards the windows and looked beyond them to where the horizon met the deep blue of the Aegean Sea. Outwardly he might appear calm, but inside his chest his heart was thudding with fury. Inside his head images were forming, memories he had thought well buried surfacing.

'I know it because they are mine,' he answered his sister, watching as her eyes widened with the shock of his disclosure.

She wasn't the only one who was shocked, Sander acknowledged. He had been shocked himself when he had looked at her phone and immediately recognised the young woman kneeling beside the two young boys who so undeniably bore the stamp of their fathering—*his* fathering. Oddly, she looked if anything younger now than she had the night he had met her in a Manchester club favoured by young footballers, and thus the haunt of the girls who chased after them. He had been taken there by a business acquaintance, who had left him to his own devices having picked up a girl himself, urging Sander to do the same.

Sander's mouth hardened. He had buried the memory of that night as deeply as he could. A one-night stand with an alcohol-fuelled girl dressed in overly tight and incredibly revealing clothes, wearing too much make-up, who had made such a deliberate play for him. At one point she had actually caught hold of his hand, as though about to drag him to bed with her. It wasn't something any real man with any pride or self-respect could ever be proud of—not even when there were the kind of extenuating circumstances there had been that night. She had been one of a clutch of such girls, openly seeking the favours of the well-paid young footballers who favoured the place. Greedy, amoral young women, whose one desire was to find themselves a rich lover or better still a rich husband. The club, he had been told, was well known for attracting such young women.

He had had sex with her out of anger and re-sentment—against her for pushing him, and against his grandfather for trying to control his life. He'd been refusing to allow him a greater say in the running of the business which, in his stubborn determination not to move with the times, he had been slowly destroying. And against his parents—his father for dying, even though that had been over a decade ago, leaving him without his support, and his mother, who had married his father out of duty whilst continuing to love another man. All those things, all that anger had welled up inside him, and the result was now here in front of him.

His sons.

His.

A feeling like nothing he had ever experienced before seized hold of him. A feeling that, until it had struck him, he would have flatly denied he would ever experience. He was a modern man—a man of logic, not emotion, and certainly not the kind of emotion he was feeling right now. Gut wrenching, instinctive, tearing at him—an emotion born of a cultural inheritance that said that a man's children, especially his sons, belonged under his roof.

Those boys were his. Their place was here with him, not in England. Here they could learn what it meant to be his sons, a Konstantinakos of Theopolis, could grow into their heritage. He could father them and guide them as his sense of responsibility demanded that he should. How much damage had they already suffered through the woman who had borne them?

He had given them life without knowing it, but now that he did know he would stop at nothing to bring them home to Theopolis, where they belonged.

CHAPTER ONE

CURSING as she heard the doorbell ring, Ruby remained where she was, on her hands and knees, hoping that whoever it was would give up and go away, leaving her in peace to get on with her cleaning. However, the bell rang again, this time almost imperiously. Someone was pressing hard on the bell.

Cursing again under her breath, Ruby backed out of the downstairs cloakroom, feeling hot and sticky, and not in any mood to have her busy blitz on cleaning whilst her twin sons were at school interrupted. She got to her feet, pushing her soft blonde curls off her face as she did so, before marching towards the front door of the house she shared with two older sisters and her own twin sons. She yanked it open.

'Look, I'm—' Her sentence went unfinished, her voice suspended by shock as she stared at the man standing on the doorstep.

Shock, disbelief, fear, anger, panic, and a sharp spear of something else that she didn't recognise exploded inside her like a fireball, with such powerful intensity that her body was drained of so much energy that she was left feeling shaky and weak, trembling inwardly beneath the onslaught of emotions.

Of course he *would* be dressed immaculately, in a dark business suit worn over a crisp blue shirt, whilst she was wearing her old jeans and a baggy tee shirt. Not that it really mattered how she looked. After all, she had no reason to want to impress him—had she? And she certainly had no reason to want him to think of her as a desirable woman, groomed and dressed for his approval. She had to clench her stomach muscles against the shudder of revulsion that threatened to betray her. The face that had haunted her dreams and then her nightmares hadn't changed—or aged. If anything he looked even more devastatingly handsome and virile than she had remembered, the dark gold gaze that had mesmerised her so effectively every bit as compelling now as it had been then. Or was it because she was a woman now and not the girl she had been that she was so immediately and shockingly aware of what a very sexual man he was? Ruby didn't know, and she didn't *want* to know.

The disbelief that had frozen her into silence had turned like snow in the sun to a dangerous slush of fear and horror inside her head—and her heart? *No!* Whatever effect he had once had on her heart, Sander Konstantinakos had no power to touch it now.

But still the small betraying word, 'You,' slid from the fullness of the naturally warm-coloured lips that had caused her parents to name her Ruby, causing a look of mixed contempt and arrogance to flash from the intense gold of Sander's eyes. Eyes the colour of the king of the jungle—as befitted a man who was in effect the ruler of the Mediterranean island that was his home.

Instinctively Ruby started to close the door on him, wanting to shut out not just Sander himself but everything he represented, but he was too quick for her, taking hold of the door and forcing it open so that he could step into the hall—and then close the door behind him, enclosing them both in the small domestic space, with its smell of cleaning fluid. Strong as it was, it still wasn't strong enough to protect her from the scent of *him*. A rash of prickly sensation raised the hairs at the back of her neck and then ran down her spine. This was ridiculous. Sander meant nothing to her now, just as she had meant nothing to him that night… But she mustn't think about that. She must concentrate instead on what she was now, not what she had been then, and she must remember the promise she had made to the twins when they had been born—she would put the past behind her.

What she had never expected was that that past would seek her out, and now it had...

'What are you doing here?' she demanded, determined to wrest control of the situation from Sander. 'What do you want?'

His mouth might be aesthetically perfect, with that well-cut top lip balancing the promise of sensuality with his fuller bottom lip, but there was nothing sensual about the tight-lipped look he was giving her, and his words were as sharply cold as the air outside the Manchester hotel in which he had abandoned her that winter morning.

'I think you know the answer to that,' he said, his English as fluent and as accentless as she remembered. 'What I want, what I have come for and what I mean to have, are my sons.'

'*Your* sons?' Fiercely proud of her twin sons, and equally fiercely maternally protective of them, there was nothing he could have said which would have been more guaranteed to arouse Ruby's anger than his verbal claim on them. Angry colour burned in the smooth perfection of Ruby's normally calm face, and her blue-green eyes were fiery with the fierce passion of her emotions.

It was over six years since this man had taken her, used her and then abandoned her as casually as though she was a…a nothing. A cheap, impulsively bought garment which in the light of day he had discarded for its cheapness. Oh, yes, she knew that she had only herself to blame for what had happened to her that fatal night. *She* had been the one to flirt with him, even if that flirtation had been alcohol-induced, and no matter how she tried to excuse her behaviour it still shamed her. But not its result—not her beautiful, adorable, much loved sons. They could never shame her, and from the moment they had been born she had been determined to be a mother of whom they could be proud—a mother with whom they could feel secure, and a mother who, no matter how much she regretted the manner in which they had been conceived, would not for one minute even want to go back in time and avoid their conception. Her sons were her life. *Her* sons.

'My sons—' she began, only to be interrupted.

'*My* sons, you mean—since in my country it is the father who has the right to claim his children, not the mother.'

'My sons were not fathered by you,' Ruby continued firmly and of course untruthfully.

'Liar,' Sander countered, reaching inside his jacket to produce a photograph which he held up in front of her.

The blood left Ruby's face. The photograph had been taken at Manchester Airport, when they had all gone to see her middle sister off on her recent flight to Italy, and the resemblance of the twins to the man who had fathered them was cruelly and undeniably revealed. The two boys were cast perfectly in their father's image, right down to the unintentionally arrogant masculine air they could adopt at times, as though deep down somewhere in their genes there was an awareness of the man who had fathered them.

Watching the colour come and go in Ruby's face, Sander allowed himself to give her a triumphant look. Of *course* the boys were his. He had known it the first second he had looked at the image on his sister's mobile phone. Their mirror image resemblance to him had sent a jolt of emotion through him unlike anything he had previously experienced.

It hadn't taken the private agency he had contacted very long to trace Ruby—although Sander had frowned over comments in the report he had received from them that implied that Ruby was a devoted mother who dedicated herself to raising her sons and was unlikely to give them up willingly. But Sander had decided that Ruby's very devotion to his sons might be the best tool he could use to ensure that she gave them up to him.

'My sons' place is with me, on the island that is their home and which ultimately will be their inheritance. Under our laws they belong to me.'

'Belong? They are children, not possessions, and no court in this country would let you take them from me.'

She was beginning to panic, but she was determined not to let him see it.

'You think not? You are living in a house that belongs to your sister, on which she has a mortgage she can no longer afford to repay, you have no money of your own, no job. No training—nothing! I, on the other hand, can provide my sons with everything that you cannot—a home, a good education, a future.'

Although she was shaken by the knowledge of how thoroughly he had done his homework, had had her investigated, Ruby was still determined to hold her ground and not allow him to overwhelm her.

'Maybe so. But can you provide them with love and the knowledge that they are truly loved and wanted? Of course you can't—because you don't love them. How can you? You don't know them.'

There—let him answer *that*! But even as she made her defiant stand Ruby's heart was warning her that Sander had raised an issue that she could not ignore and would ultimately have to face. Honesty compelled her to admit it.

'I do know that one day they will want to know who fathered them and what their family history is,' she said.

It was hard for her to make that admission—just as it had been hard for her to answer the questions the boys had already asked, saying that they did have a daddy but he lived in a different country. Those words had reminded her of what she was denying her sons because of the circumstances in which she had conceived them. One day, though, their questions would be those of teenagers, not little boys, and far more searching, far more knowing.

Ruby looked away from Sander, instinctively

wanting to hide her inner fears from him. The problem of telling the boys how she had come to have them lay across her heart and her conscience in an ever present heavy weight. At the moment they simply accepted that, like many of the other children they were at school with, they did not have a daddy living with them. But one day they would start to ask more questions, and she had hoped desperately that she would not have to tell them the truth until they were old enough to accept it without judging her. Now Sander had stirred up all the anxieties she had tried to put to one side. More than anything else she wanted to be a good mother, to give her boys the gift of a secure childhood filled with love; she wanted them to grow up knowing they were loved, confident and happy, without the burden of having to worry about adult relationships. For that reason she was determined never, ever to begin a relationship with anyone. A changing parade of 'uncles' and 'stepfathers' wasn't what she wanted for her boys.

But now Sander, with his demands and his questions, was forcing her to think about the future and her sons' reactions to the reality of their conception. The fact that they did not have a father who loved them.

Anger and panic swirled through her.

'Why are you doing this?' she demanded. 'The boys mean nothing to you. They are five years old, and you didn't even know that they existed until now.'

'That is true. But as for them meaning nothing to me—you are wrong. They are of my blood, and that alone means that I have a responsibility to ensure that they are brought up within their family.'

He wasn't going to tell her about that atavistic surge of emotion and connection he had felt the minute he had seen the twins' photograph. Sander still didn't really understand it himself. He only knew that it had brought him here, and that it would keep him here until she handed over to him his sons.

'It can't have been easy for you financially, bringing them up.'

Sander was offering her sympathy? Ruby was immediately suspicious. She longed to tell him that what *hadn't* been easy for her was discovering at seventeen that she was pregnant by a man who had slept with her and then left her, but somehow she managed to resist doing so.

Sander gestured round the hall.

'Even if your sister is able to keep up the mortgage payments on this house, have you thought about what would happen if either of your sisters wanted to marry and move out? At the moment you are financially dependent on their goodwill. As a caring mother, naturally you will want your sons to have the best possible education and a comfortable life. I can provide them with both, and provide you with the money to live your own life. It can't be much fun for you, tied to two small children all the time.'

She had been right to be suspicious, Ruby recognised, as the full meaning of Sander's offer hit her. Did he really expect her to *sell* her sons to him? Didn't he realise how obscene his offer was? Or did he simply not care?

His determination made her cautious in her response, her instincts warning her to be careful about any innocent admission she might make as to the financial hardship they were all currently going through, in case Sander tried to use that information against her at a later date. So, instead of reacting with the anger she felt, she said instead, 'The twins are only five. Now that they're at school I'm planning to continue my education. As for me having fun—the boys provide me with all the fun I want or need.'

'You'll forgive me if I say that I find that hard to believe, given the circumstances under which we met,' was Sander's smooth and cruel response.

'That was six years ago, and in circumstances that—' Ruby broke off. Why should she explain herself to him? The people closest to her—her sisters—knew and understood what had driven her to the reckless behaviour that had resulted in the twins' conception, and their love and support for her had never wavered. She owed Sander nothing after all—much less the revelation of her teenage vulnerabilities. 'That was then,' she corrected herself, adding firmly, 'This is now.'

The knowing look Sander was giving her made Ruby want to protest—*You're wrong. I'm not what you think. That wasn't the real me that night.* But common sense and pride made her hold back the words.

'I'm prepared to be very generous to you financially in return for you handing the twins over to me,' Sander continued. 'Very generous indeed. You're still young.'

In fact he had been surprised to discover that the night they had met she had been only seventeen. Dressed and made-up as she had been, he had assumed that she was much older. Sander frowned. He hadn't enjoyed the sharp spike of distaste he had experienced against himself at knowing he had taken such a young girl to bed. Had he known her age he would have… What? Given her a stern talking to and sent her home in a cab? Had he been in control of himself that night he would not have gone to bed with her at all, no matter what her age, but the unpalatable truth was that he had *not* been in control of himself. He had been in the grip of anger and a sense of frustration he had never experienced either before or since that night—a firestorm of savage, bitter emotion that had driven him into behaviour that, if he was honest, still irked his pride and sense of self. Other men might exhibit such behaviour, but he had always thought of himself as above that kind of thing. He had been wrong, and now the evidence of that behaviour was confronting him in the shape of the sons he had fathered. Sander believed he had a duty to ensure that they did not suffer because of that behaviour. That was what had brought him here. And there was no way he was going to leave until he had got what he had come for.

And just that?

Ruby shook her head.

'Buy my children, you mean?'

Sander could hear the hostility in Ruby's voice as well as see it in her eyes.

'Because that *is* what you're talking about,' Ruby accused him, adding fiercely, 'And if I'd had any thought of allowing you into their lives, what you've just said would make me change my mind. There's nothing you could offer me that would make me want to risk my sons' emotional future by allowing *you* to have any kind of contact with them.'

Her words were having more of an effect on him than Sander liked to admit. A man of pride and power, used to commanding not just the obedience but also the respect and the admiration of others, he was stung by Ruby's criticism of him. He wasn't used to being refused anything by anyone—much less by a woman he remembered as an over-made-up and under-dressed little tart who had come on to him openly and obviously. Not that there was anything of that girl about her now, dressed in faded jeans and a loose top, her face free of make-up and her hair left to curl naturally of its own accord. The girl he remembered had smelled of cheap scent; the woman in front of him smelled of cleaning product. He would have to change his approach if he was to overcome her objections, Sander recognised.

Quickly changing tack, he challenged her. 'Nothing I could offer *you*, maybe, but what about what I can offer my sons? You speak of their emotions. Have you thought, I wonder, how they are going to feel when they grow up to realise what you have denied them in refusing to let them know their father?'

'That's not fair,' Ruby objected angrily, knowing that Sander had found her most vulnerable spot where the twins were concerned.

'What is not fair, surely, is you denying my sons the opportunity to know their father and the culture that is their birthright?'

'As your bastards?' The horrible word tasted bitter, but it had to be said. 'Forced to stand in second place to your legitimate children, and no doubt be resented by your wife?'

'I have no other children, nor any wife.'

Why was her heart hammering so heavily, thudding into her chest wall? It didn't matter to her whether or not Sander was married, did it?

'I warn you now, Ruby, that I intend to have my sons with me. Whatever it takes to achieve that and by whatever means.'

Ruby's mouth went dry. Stories she had read about children being kidnapped by a parent and stolen away out of the country flooded into her mind. Sander was a very rich and a very powerful man. She had discovered that in the early days after she had met him, when she had stupidly imagined that he would come back to her and had avidly read everything she could about him, wanting to learn everything she could—until the reality of the situation had forced her to accept that the fantasy she had created of Sander marrying her and looking after her was just that: a fantasy created by her need to find someone to replace the parents she had lost and keep her safe.

It was true that Sander could give the boys far more than she could materially, and the unwelcome thought slid into her mind that there could come a day when, as Sander had cruelly predicted, the twins might actually resent her and blame her for preventing them from benefitting from their father's wealth and, more importantly, from knowing him. Boys needed a strong male figure in their lives they could relate to. Everyone knew that. Secretly she had been worrying about the lack of any male influence in their lives. But if at times she had been tempted to pray for a solution to that problem she had certainly not envisaged that solution coming in the form of the boys' natural father. A kindly, grandfather-type figure for them was as much as she had hoped for, because after their birth she had decided that she would never take the risk of getting involved with a man who might turn out to be only a temporary presence in her sons' lives. She would rather remain celibate than risk that.

The truth, in her opinion, was that children thrived best with two parents in a stable relationship—a mother and a father, both committed to their wellbeing.

A mother and a father. More than most, she knew the damage that could be done when that stability wasn't there.

A sense of standing on the edge of a precipice filled her—an awareness that the decision she made now would affect her sons for the rest of their lives. Shakily she admitted to herself that she wished her sisters were there to help her, but they weren't. They had their own lives, and ultimately the boys were *her* responsibility, their happiness resting in *her* hands. Sander was determined to have them. He had said so. He was a wealthy, powerful and charismatic man who would have no difficulty whatsoever in persuading others that the boys should be with him. But she was their mother. She couldn't let him take them from her—for their sakes even more than her own. Sander didn't love them; he merely wanted them. She doubted he was capable of understanding what love was. Yes, he would provide well for them materially, but children needed far more than that, and her sons needed *her*. She had raised them from birth; they needed her even more than she needed them.

If she couldn't stop Sander from claiming his sons, then she owed it to them to make sure that she remained with them. Sander wouldn't want that, of course. He despised and disliked her.

Her heart started to thud uncomfortably heavily and far too fast as it fought against the solution proposed by her brain, but now that the thought was there it couldn't be ignored. Sander had said there was nothing he would not do to have his sons living with him. Well, maybe she should put his claim to the test, because she knew that there was no sacrifice she herself would not make for their sakes—no sacrifice at all. The challenge she intended to put to him was a huge risk for her to take, but for the boys' sake she was prepared to take it. It was, after all, a challenge she was bound to win—because Sander would never accept the terms with which she was about to confront him. She was sure of that. She let out her pent up breath.

'You say the boys' place is with you?'

'It is.'

'They are five years old and I am their mother.' Ruby took a deep breath, hoping that her voice wouldn't shake with the nervousness she was fighting to suppress and thus betray her. 'If you really care about their wellbeing as much as you claim then you must know that they are too young to be separated from me.'

She had a point, Sander was forced to admit, even though he didn't like doing so.

'You need to be very sure about why you want the twins, Sander.' Ruby pressed home her point.

'And that your desire to have them isn't merely a rich man's whim. Because the only way I will allow them to be with you is if I am there with them—as their mother and your wife.'

CHAPTER TWO

THERE—she had said it. Thrown down the gauntlet, so to speak, and given him her challenge.

In the silence that followed Ruby could literally hear her own heart beating as she held her breath, waiting for Sander to refuse her demand—because she knew that he *would* refuse it, and having refused it he must surely be forced to step back and accept that the boys' place was with her.

Trying not to give in to the shakiness invading her body, Ruby could hardly believe that she had actually had the courage to say what she had. She could tell from Sander's expression that her demand had shocked him, although he was quick to mask his reaction.

Marriage, Sander thought quickly, mentally assessing his options. He wanted his sons. There was no doubt in his mind about that, nor any doubt that they were his. Marriage to their mother would give him certain rights over them, but it would also give Ruby certain rights over his wealth. That, of course, was exactly what she wanted. Marriage to him followed by an equally speedy divorce and a very generous financial divorce settlement. He could read her mind so easily. Even so, she had caught him off-guard—although he told himself cynically that he should perhaps have been prepared for her demand. He was, after all, a very wealthy man.

'I applaud your sharp-witted business acu-men,' he told Ruby drily, in a neutral voice that gave away nothing of the fury he was really feeling. 'You rejected my initial offer of a generous payment under the guise of being a devoted mother, when in reality you were already planning to play for higher stakes.'

'That's not true,' Ruby denied hotly, astonished by his interpretation of her demand. 'Your money means nothing to me, Sander— nothing at all,' she told him truthfully, adding for good measure, 'And neither do you. For me, the fact that you choose to think of my offer in terms of money simply underlines all the reasons why I am not prepared to allow my sons anywhere near you unless I am there.'

'That is how *you* feel, but what about how *they* might feel?' Sander pressed her. 'A good mother would never behave so selfishly. She would put her children's interests first.'

How speedily Sander had turned the tables on her, Ruby recognised. What had begun as a challenge to him she had been confident would make him back down had now turned into a double-edged sword which right now he was wielding very skilfully against her, cutting what she had thought was secure ground away from under her feet.

'They need their mother—' she started.

'They are *my* sons,' Sander interrupted her

angrily. 'And I mean to have them. If I have to marry you to facilitate that, then so be it. But make no mistake, Ruby. I intend to have my sons.'

His response stunned her. She had been expecting him to refuse, to back down, to go away and leave them alone—anything rather than marry her. Sander had called her bluff and left her defenceless.

Now Ruby could see a reality she hadn't seen before. Sander really did want the boys and he meant to have them. He was rich and powerful, well able to provide materially for his sons. What chance would she have of keeping them if he pursued her through the courts? At best all she could hope for was shared custody, with the boys passed to and fro between them, torn between two homes, and that was the last thing she wanted for them. *Why* had Sander had to discover that he had fathered them? Hadn't life been cruel enough to her as it was?

Marriage to him, which she had not in any kind of way wanted, had now devastatingly turned into the protection she was forced to recognise she might need if she was to continue to have the permanent place in her sons' lives that she had previously taken for granted.

Marriage to Sander wouldn't just provide her sons with a father, she recognised now through growing panic, it would also protect her rights as a mother. As long as they were married the twins would have both parents there for them.

Both parents. Ruby swallowed painfully. Wasn't it true that she had spent many sleepless nights worrying about the future and the effect not having a father figure might have on her sons?

A father figure, but not their real father. She had *never* imagined them having Sander in their lives—not after those first agonising weeks of being forced to accept that she meant nothing to him.

She wasn't going to give up, though. She would fight with every bit of her strength for her sons.

Holding her head up she told him fiercely, 'Very well, then. The choice is yours, Sander.

If you genuinely want the boys because they are your sons, and because you want to get to know them and be part of their lives, then you will accept that separating them from me will inflict huge emotional damage on them. You will understand, as I do, no matter how much that understanding galls you, that children need the security of having two parents they know are there for them—will always be there for them. You will be prepared to make the same sacrifice that I am prepared to make to provide them with the security that comes from having two parents committed to them and to each other through marriage.'

'Sacrifice?' Sander demanded. 'I am a billionaire. I don't think there are many women who would consider marriage to me a *sacrifice*.'

Did he really believe that? If so, it just showed how right she was to want to ensure that her sons grew up knowing there were far more important things in life than money.

'You are very cynical,' she told him. 'There

are any number of women who would be appalled by what you have just said—women who put love before money, women like me who put their children first, women who would run from a man like you. I don't want your money, and I am quite willing to sign a document saying so.'

'Oh, you will be doing that. Make no mistake about it,' Sander assured her ruthlessly. Did she really expect him to fall for her lies and her faked lack of interest in his money? 'There is no way I will abandon my sons to the care of a mother who could very soon be without a roof over her head—a mother who would have to rely on charity in order to feed and clothe them—a mother who dressed like a tart and offered herself to a man she didn't know.'

Ruby flinched as though he had physically hit her, but she still managed to ask quickly, 'Were *you* any better? Or does the fact that you are a man and I'm a woman somehow mean that my behaviour was worse than yours? I was a seventeen-year-old-girl; you were an adult male.'

A seventeen-year-old girl. Angered by the reminder, Sander reacted against it. 'You certainly weren't dressed like a schoolgirl—or an innocent. And you were the one who propositioned me, not the other way round.'

And now he was going to be forced to marry her. Sander didn't want to marry anyone—much less a woman like her.

What he had seen in his parents' marriage, the bitterness and resentment between them, had made him vow never to marry himself. That vow had been the cause of acrimony and dissent between him and his grandfather, a despot who believed he had the right to barter his own flesh and blood in marriage as though they were just another part of his fleet of tankers.

Refusing Ruby's proposal would give her an advantage. She could and would undoubtedly attempt to use his refusal against him were there to be a court case between them over the twins.

But her obstinacy and her attempt to get the better of him had hardened Sander's determination to claim his sons—even if it now meant using underhand methods to do so. Once they were on his island, its laws would ensure that he, as their father, had the right to keep them.

The familiar sound of a car drawing up outside and doors opening had Ruby ignoring Sander to hurry to the door. She suddenly realised what time it was, and that the twins were being dropped off by the neighbour with whom she shared school run duties. Opening the door, she hurried down the drive to thank her neighbour and help the twins out of the car, gathering up school bags and lunchboxes as she did, clucking over the fact that neither boy had fastened his coat despite the fact that it was still only March and cold.

Identical in every way, except for the tiny mole behind Freddie's right ear, the boys stood and stared at the expensive car parked on the drive, and then looked at Ruby.

'Whose car is that?' Freddie asked, round-eyed.

Ruby couldn't answer him. Why hadn't she realised the time and got rid of Sander before the twins came home from school? Now they were bound to ask questions—questions she wasn't going to be able to answer honestly—and she hated the thought of lying to them.

Freddie was still waiting for her to answer. Forcing a reassuring smile, she told him, 'It's just…someone's. Come on, let's get inside before the two of you catch cold with your coats unfastened like that.'

'I'm hungry. Can we have toast with peanut butter?' Harry asked her hopefully.

Peanut butter was his current favourite.

'We'll see,' was Ruby's answer as she pushed then gently into the hall in front of her. 'Upstairs now, boys,' she told them both, trying to remain as calm as she could even as they stood and stared in silence at Sander, who now seemed to be taking up a good deal of space in the hallway.

He was tall, well over six foot, and in other circumstances it would have made her smile to see the way Harry tipped his head right back to look up at him. Freddie, though, suddenly very much the man of the family as the elder of the two. He moved closer to her, as if instinctively seeking to protect her, and some silent communication between the two of them caused his twin to fall back to her other side to do the same.

Unwanted emotional tears stung Ruby's eyes. Her darling boys. They didn't deserve any of this, and it was *her* fault that things were as they were. Before she could stop herself she dropped down on one knee, putting an arm around each twin, holding them to her. Freddie was the more sensitive of the two, although he tried to conceal it, and he turned into her immediately, burying his face in her neck and holding her tightly, whilst Harry looked briefly towards Sander—wanting to go to him? Ruby wondered wretchedly—before copying his brother.

Sander couldn't move. The second he had seen the two boys he had known that there was nothing he would not do for them—including tearing out his own heart and offering it to them on a plate. The sheer force of his love for them was like a tidal wave, a tsunami that swept everything else aside. They were his—of his family, of his blood, of his body. They were his. And yet, watching them, he recognised immediately how they felt about their mother. He had seen the protective stance they had taken up and his heart filled with pride to see that instinctive maleness in them.

An old memory stirred within him: strong sunlight striking down on his bare head, the raised angry voices of his parents above him. He too had turned to his mother, as his sons had turned to theirs, but there had been no loving maternal arms to hold him. Instead his mother had spun round, heading for her car, slamming the door after she'd climbed into it, leaving him behind, tyres spinning on the gravel, sending up a shower of small stones. He had turned then to his father, but he too had turned away from him and walked back to the house. His parents had been too caught up in their own lives and their resentment of one another to have time for him.

Sander looked down at his sons—and at their mother.

They were all their sons had. He thought again of his own parents, and realised on another surge of emotion that there was nothing he would not do to give his sons what he had never had.

'Marriage it is, then. But I warn you now it will be a marriage that will last for life. That is the measure of my commitment to them,' he told her, looking at the boys.

If she hadn't been holding the twins Ruby thought she might well have fallen down in shock—shock and dismay. She searched Sander's face for some sign that he didn't really mean what he was saying, but all she could see was a quiet, implacable determination.

The twins were turning in her arms to look at

Sander again. Any moment now they would start asking questions.

'Upstairs, you two,' she repeated, taking off their navy duffel coats. 'Change out of your uniforms and then wash your hands.'

They made a dash past Sander, deliberately ignoring him, before climbing the stairs together—a pair of sturdy, healthy male children, with lean little-boy bodies and their father's features beneath identical mops of dark curls.

'There will be two conditions,' Sander continued coldly. 'The first is that you will sign a prenuptial agreement. Our marriage will be for the benefit of our sons, not the benefit of your bank account.'

Appalled and hurt by this fresh evidence of how little he thought of her, Ruby swallowed her pride—she was doing this for her boys, after all—and demanded through gritted teeth, 'And the second condition?'

'Your confirmation and proof that you are taking the birth control pill. I've seen the evidence of how little care you have for such matters. I have no wish for another child to be conceived as carelessly as the twins were.'

Now Ruby was too outraged to conceal her feelings.

'There is no question of that happening. The last thing I want is to have to share your bed again.'

She dared to claim *that*, after the way she had already behaved?

Her outburst lashed Sander's pride into a savage need to punish her.

'But you *will* share it, and you will beg me to satisfy that hunger in you I have already witnessed. Your desire for sexual satisfaction has been honed in the arms of far too many men for you to be able to control it now.'

'No! That's not true.'

Ruby could feel her face burning. She didn't need reminding about the wanton way in which she had not only given herself to him but actively encouraged him to take her. Her memories of that night were burned into her conscience for ever. Not one of her senses would ever forget the role they had played in her self-humiliation—the way her voice had sobbed and risen on an increasing note of aching longing that had resulted in a cry of abandoned pleasure that still echoed in her ears, the greedy need of her hands to touch and know his body, the hunger of her lips to caress his flesh and taste his kisses, the increased arousal the scent of his skin had brought her. Each and all of them had added to a wild torrent of sexual longing that had taken her to the edge of her universe and then beyond it, to a place of such spectacular loss of self that she never wanted to go there again.

Shaking herself free of the memories threatening to deluge her, Ruby returned staunchly, 'That was different...a mistake.' Her hands curled into her palms in bitter self-defence as she saw the cynical look he was giving her. 'And it's one that I never want to repeat.

There's no way I'd ever want to share your bed again.'

Her denial unleashed Sander's anger. She was lying, he was sure of it, and he would prove it to her. He wasn't a vain man, but he knew that women found him attractive, and Ruby had certainly done everything she could that night to make it plain to him that she wanted him. Normally he would never have even considered bedding her—he liked to do his own hunting—but her persistence had been like a piece of grit in his shoe, wearing down his resistance and helping to fuel the anger already burning inside him. *That* was why he had lost control. Because of his grandfather. Not because of Ruby herself, or because the aroused little cries she had made against his skin had proved so irresistible that he had lost sight of everything but his need to possess her. He could still remember the way she had cried out when he had finally thrust into her, as though what she was experiencing was completely new to her. She had clung to him, sobbing her pleasure into his skin as she trembled and shuddered against him.

Why was he thinking of that now?

The savagery of his fury, inflamed by both her demand for marriage and her denial of his accusation, deafened him to the note of raw pain in her voice. Before he could stop himself he had taken hold of her and was possessing her mouth in a kiss of scorching, pride-fuelled fury.

Too shocked to struggle against his possession, by the time she realised what was happening it was too late. Ruby's own anger surged in defiance, passionate enough to overwhelm her self-control and battle with the full heat of Sander's desire to punish her. Desire for him was the last thing she had expected to feel, but, shockingly, the hard possession of Sander's mouth on her own turned a key in a lock she had thought so damaged by what he had already made her endure that it could never be turned again. Turned it with frightening ease.

This shouldn't be happening. It could not be happening. But, shamefully, it was.

Her panic fought with the desire that burned through her and lost, overcome as swiftly as though molten lava was pouring through her, obliterating everything that stood in its path. Her lips parted beneath the driving pressure of Sander's probing tongue, an agonised whimper of longing drawn from her throat. She could feel the passion in Sander's kiss, and the hard arousal of his body, but instead of acting as a warning that knowledge only served to further enflame her own desire, quickening the pulse already beating within her own sex.

Somewhere within the torrent of anger motivating him Sander could hear an inner voice warning him that this was how it had been before—this same furious, aching, agonised need and arousal that was possessing him now. It should have been impossible for him to want her. It should always have been impossible. And yet, like some mythical, dark malformed creature, supposedly entombed and shut away for ever, his desire had found the superhuman strength to break the bonds imprisoning it. His tongue possessed the eager willingness of the softness of her mouth and his body was already hard, anticipating the corresponding willingness of the most intimate part of her if he didn't stop soon…

Ruby shuddered with mindless sensual delight as Sander's tongue began to thrust potently and rhythmically against her own. Beneath her clothes her nipples swelled and hardened, their ache spreading swiftly through her. Sander's hand cupped her breast, causing her to moan deep in her throat.

She was all female sensual heat, all eager willingness, her very responsiveness designed to trap, Sander recognised. If he didn't stop now he wouldn't be able to stop himself from taking her where they stood, from dragging the clothes from her body in his need to feel her bare skin against his touch, from sinking himself deep within her and feeling her body close round him, possessing him as he possessed her, both of them driven by the mindless, incessant ache that he was surely cursed to feel for her every time he touched her.

He found the buttons on her shirt, swiftly unfastening them. The feel of his hands on her body drew Ruby back into the past. Then he had undressed her expertly and swiftly, in between sensually erotic kisses that had melted away her ability to think or reason, leaving her aching for more, just as he was doing now. His left hand lifted her hair so that he could taste the warm sweetness of that place just where her neck joined her shoulder.

Ruby felt the warmth of his breath against her bare skin. Flames were erupting inside her—the eager flames of denied longing leaping upwards, consuming her resistance. Mindless shudders of hot pleasure rippled through her. Her shirt was open, her breasts exposed to Sander's gaze.

He shouldn't be doing this, Sander warned

himself. He shouldn't be giving in to the demands of his pride. But that was *all* he was doing. The heat running through his veins was only caused by angry pride, nothing else.

Her breasts were as perfect as he remembered, the dark rose nipples flaring into deep aureoles that contrasted with the paleness of her skin. He watched as they lifted and fell with the increased speed of her breathing, lifting his hand to cup one, knowing already that it would fit his hand as perfectly as though it was made to be held by him. Beneath the stroke of his thumb-pad her nipple hardened. Sander closed his eyes, remembering how in that long-ago hotel bedroom it had seemed as though her nipple was pushing itself against his touch, demanding the caress of first his thumb and forefinger, then his lips and tongue. Her response had been wild and immediate, swelling and hardening his own body.

He didn't want her, not really, but his pride

was now demanding her punishment, the destruction of her claim that she didn't want him.

Ruby could feel herself being dragged back to the past. A small cry of protest gave away her torment.

Abruptly Sander thrust her away from him, brought back to reality by the sound.

They stood watching one another, fighting to control the urgency of their breathing, the urgency of their need. Exposed, raw, and in Ruby's eyes ugly, it was almost a tangible force between them.

They both felt the strength of it and its danger. Ruby could see that knowledge in Sander's eyes, just as she knew he must see it reflected in her own.

The weight of her shame ached through her.

Ruby's face was drained of colour, her eyes huge with shock in her small face.

Sander was just as shocked by the intensity of the desire that had come out of nowhere to threaten his self-control—but he was better at hiding it than Ruby, and he was in no mood to find any pity for her. He was still battling with the unwanted knowledge of just how much he had wanted her.

'You will take the contraceptive pill,' he told her coldly. His heart started to pound heavily in recognition of what his words meant and invited, and the ache in his body surged against his self-control, but somehow he forced himself to ignore the demands of his own desire, to continue. 'I will not accept any consequences of you not doing so.'

Never had she felt so weak, Ruby thought shakily—and not just physically weak, but emotionally and mentally weak as well. In the space of a few short minutes the protective cover she had woven around herself had been ripped from her, exposing her to the full horror of a weakness she had thought controlled and contained. It should be impossible for her to want Sander, to be aroused by him. Should be.

Reaction to what had happened was setting in.

She felt physically sick, dazed, unable to function properly, torn apart by the conflicting nature of her physical desire and her burning sense of shame and disbelief that she should feel that desire… Wild thoughts jostled through her head. Perhaps she should not merely ask her doctor for a prescription for the birth control pill but for an anti-Sander pill as well—something that would destroy her desire for him? She needed a pill for that? Surely the way he had spoken to her, the way he had treated her, should be enough to ensure that she loathed the thought of him touching her? Surely her pride and the humiliation he had heaped on her should be strong enough to protect her?

She couldn't marry him. Not now. Panic filled her.

'I've changed my mind,' she told him quickly. 'About…about us getting married.'

Sander frowned. His immediate response to her statement was a fierce surge of determination to prevent her from changing her mind. For the sake of his sons. Nothing else. And certainly not because of the ache that was still pounding through him.

'So the future of our sons is not as important to you as you claimed after all?' he challenged her.

She was trapped, Ruby acknowledged, trapped in a prison of her own making. All she could do was cling to the fragile hope that somehow she would find the strength to deny the desire he could arouse in her so easily.

'Of course it is,' she protested.

'Then we shall be married, and you will accept my terms and conditions.'

'And if I refuse?'

'Then I will move heaven and earth and the stars between them to take my sons from you.'

He meant what he was saying, Ruby could tell. She had no choice other than to bow her head in acceptance of his demands.

He had defeated her, Sander knew, but the taste of his triumph did not have the sweetness he had expected.

'The demands placed on me by my business mean that the sooner the arrangements are completed the better. I shall arrange for the necessary paperwork to be carried out with regard to the prenuptial agreement I shall require you to sign and for our marriage. You must—'

A sudden bang from upstairs, followed by a sharp cry of pain, had them both turning towards the stairs.

Anxious for the safety of her sons, Ruby rushed past Sander, hurrying up the stairs to the boys' room, unaware that Sander was right behind her as she pushed open the door to find Harry on the floor sobbing whilst Freddie stood clutching one of their toy cars.

'Freddie pushed me,' Harry told her.

'No, I didn't. He was trying to take my car.'

'Let me have a look,' Ruby instructed Harry, quickly checking to make sure that no real damage had been done before sitting back on her heels and turning to look at Freddie. But instead of coming to her for comfort Freddie was standing in front of Sander, who had obviously followed her into the room, looking up at him as though seeking his support, and Sander had his hand on Freddie's arm, as though protecting him.

The raw intensity of her emotions gripped her by the throat—grief for all that the twins had missed in not having a father, guilt because she was the cause of that, pain because she loved them so much but her love alone could not give them the tools they would need to grow into well balanced men, and fear for her own self-respect.

His hand resting protectively on the shoulder of his son, Sander looked grimly at Ruby. His sons needed him in their lives, and nothing— least of all a woman like Ruby—was going to prevent him from being there for them.

Oblivious to the atmosphere between the two grown-ups Freddie repeated, 'It's *my* car.'

'No, it's not. It's mine,' Harry argued.

Their argument pulled Ruby's attention back

to them. They were devoted to one another, but every now and again they would argue like this over a toy, as though each of them was trying to seek authority over the other. It was a boy thing, other mothers had assured her, but Ruby hated to see them fall out.

'I've got a suggestion to make.' Sander's voice was calm, and yet authoritative in a way that immediately had both boys looking at him. 'If you both promise not to argue over this car again then I will buy you a new toy each, so you won't have to share.'

Ruby sucked in an outraged breath, her maternal instincts overwhelming the vulnerability she felt towards Sander as a woman. What he was doing was outright bribery. Since she didn't have the money to give the boys one each of things she had impressed on them the need to share and share alike, and now, with a handful of words, Sander had appealed to their natural acquisitive instincts with his offer.

She could see from the eager look in both

pairs of dark gold eyes that her rules about sharing had been forgotten even before Harry challenged Sander excitedly, 'When…when can we have them?'

Harry was on his feet now, rushing over to join his twin and lean confidently against Sander's other leg whilst he looked up excitedly at him, his words tumbling over themselves as he told Sander, 'I want a car like the one outside…'

'So do I,' Freddie agreed, determined not to be outdone and to assert his elder brother status.

'I'm taking both of you and your mother to London.'

This was news to Ruby, but she wasn't given the chance to say anything because Sander was already continuing.

'There's a big toyshop there where we can look for your cars—but only if you promise me not to quarrel over your toys in future.'

Two dark heads nodded enthusiastically in assent, and two identical watermelon grins split her sons' faces as they gazed up worship-fully at Sander.

Ruby struggled to contain her feelings. Seeing her sons with Sander, watching the way they reacted to him, had brought home to her more effectively than a thousand arguments could ever have done just what they were missing without him—not financially, but emotionally.

Was it her imagination, or was she right in thinking that already they seemed to be standing taller, speaking more confidently, even displaying a body language they had automatically copied from their father? A small pang of sadness filled her. They weren't babies any longer, *her* babies, wholly dependent on her for everything; they were growing up, and their reaction to Sander proved what she had already known—they needed a male role model in their lives. Helplessly she submitted to the power of the wave of maternal love that surged through her, but her head lifted proudly as she returned Sander's silently challenging look.

Automatically Ruby reached out to stroke the tousled dark curls exactly at the moment that Sander did the same. Their hands touched. Immediately Ruby recoiled from the contact, unable to stop the swift rush of knowledge that slid into her head. Once Sander's hands had touched her far more intimately than they were doing now, taking her and possessing her with a potent mix of knowledge and male arousal, and something else which in her ignorance and innocence she had told herself was passionate desire for her and her alone, but which of course had been nothing of the sort.

That reality had left her emotions badly bruised. His was the only sexual male touch she had ever known. Memories she had thought sealed away for ever were trying to surface. Memories aroused by that kiss Sander had forced on her earlier. Ruby shuddered in mute loathing of her own weakness, but it was too late. The mental images her memories were painting would not be denied—images of Sander's hands on her body, the sound of his breathing against her ear and then later her skin. But, no, she must not think of those things. Instead she must be strong. She must resist and deny his ability to arouse her. She was not that young girl any more, she was a woman, a mother, and her sons' needs must come before her own.

CHAPTER THREE

RUBY'S head was pounding with a tension headache, and her stomach cramped—familiar reactions to stress, which she knew could well result in her ending up with something close to a full-scale migraine attack. But this wasn't the time for her to be ill, or indeed to show any weakness—even if she had hardly slept since and had woken this morning feeling nauseous.

The twins were dressed in the new jumpers and jeans her sisters had bought them for Christmas, and wearing the new trainers she had spent her preciously saved money on after she had seen the frowning look Sander had given their old ones when he had called to discuss everything—'everything' being all the arrangements he had made, not just for their stay in London but for their marriage as well, before the four of them would leave for the island that would be their home. They were too excited to sit down, insisting instead on standing in front of the window so that they could see Sander arrive to pick them all up for their visit to London.

Would she have made a different decision if her sisters had been at home? Ruby didn't see how she could have done. They had been wonderful to her, insisting that they would support her financially so that she could stay at home with the boys, but Ruby had become increasingly aware not just of the financial pressure they were under, but also the fact that one day surely her sisters would fall in love. When they did she didn't want to feel she and the twins were standing in their way because they felt duty-bound to go on supporting them.

No, she had made the right decision. For the twins, who were both wildly excited about the coming trip to London and who had happily accepted her careful announcement to them that she was going to marry Sander, and for her sisters, who had given her and the twins so much love and support.

The twins had reacted to the news that she and Sander were going to be married with excitement and delight, and Freddie had informed her hopefully, 'Luke Simpson has a daddy. He takes him to watch football, and to McDonalds, and he bought him a new bicycle.'

The reality was that everything seemed to be working in Sander's favour. She couldn't even use the excuse of saying that she couldn't take the boys out of school to refuse to go to London, since they were now on holiday for Easter.

When they went back to school it would be to the small English speaking school on the island where, Sander had informed her, those islanders who wished their children to grow up speaking English could send them.

The conversation she and Sander had had

about the twins' future had been more of a question and answer session, with her asking the questions and Sander supplying the answers. All she knew about their future life was that Sander preferred to live and work on the island his family had ruled for several centuries, although the container shipping business he had built up into a worldwide concern also had offices and staff at all the world's major commercial ports, including Felixstowe in England. Sander had also told her that his second in command was his younger brother, who had trained in IT and was based in Athens.

When it came to the boys' future education, Sander had told her that he was completely against them going to boarding school—much to her own relief. He had said that when the time came they would spend term time in England as a family, returning to the island when the boys were out of school.

In addition to the younger brother, Sander had informed her, he also had a sister—the same sister Ruby had learned had taken the photograph of the twins that had alerted Sander to their existence. Like his brother, she too lived in Athens with her husband.

'So it will just be the two of us and the boys, then?' she had pressed warily.

'That is the norm, isn't it?' he had countered. 'The nuclear family, comprising a father, a mother and their children.'

Stupidly, perhaps, she hadn't thought as far as how they would live, but the way her thoughts had recoiled from the reality of their new life together had shown her how apprehensive she was. Because she feared him, or because she feared wanting him? Her face burned even now, remembering her inability to answer that inner question.

It had been far easier to deal with the practicalities of what lay ahead rather than allow herself to be overwhelmed by the complex emotional issues it raised.

Now, waiting for Sander to collect them, with

letters for her sisters explaining what she was doing and why written and waiting for them on their return to the UK—the situation wasn't something she felt she wanted to discuss with them over the phone—Ruby could feel the pain in her temple increasing, whilst her stomach churned with anxiety. Everything would have been so very different if only she hadn't give in to that shameful physical desire Sander had somehow managed to arouse in her. In her handbag were the birth control pills Sander had demanded that she take. She had been tempted to defy him, to insist that she could rely on her own willpower to ensure that there was no further sexual intimacy between them. But she was still horrified by the memory of what had happened between them in her hallway, still struggling to take in the fact that it had happened. The speed of it, the intensity of it, had been like a fire erupting out of nowhere to blaze so fiercely that it was beyond control. It had left her feeling vulnerable and unable to trust herself.

There must not be another child, Sander had told her. And wasn't the truth that she herself did not *want* to create another new life with a man who had no respect for her, no feelings of kindness towards her, and certainly no love for her? Love? Hadn't she grown out of the dangerous self-deceit of dressing up naked lust in the fantasy illusion of 'love'? Clothing it in the kind of foolish dreams that belonged to naive adolescents? Before Sander had kissed her she would have sworn and believed that there was nothing he could do to her, no intimacy he could enforce on her, that would arouse her own desire. But the searing heat of the kiss he had subjected her to had burned away her defences.

She hated having to admit to herself that she couldn't rely on her own pride and self-control, but the only thing she could cling to was the knowledge that Sander had been as close to losing *his* control as she had been of losing hers. Of all the cruel tricks that nature could play on two human beings, surely that must be the worst? To create within them a desire for one another that could burn away every shred of protection, leaving them exposed to a need that neither of them wanted. If she could have ripped her own desire out of her body she would have done. It was an alien, unwanted presence, an enemy within her that she must find a way to destroy.

'He's here!'

Freddie's excited announcement cut through her introspection. Both boys were racing to the door and pulling it open, jumping up and down with eager delight when the car door opened and Sander stepped out.

He might be dressed casually, in a black polo shirt, beige chinos and a dark tan leather jacket, but Sander still had that unmistakable air about him that said he was a man other men looked up to and women wanted to be close to, Ruby was forced to admit unwillingly. It wasn't just that he was good-looking—many men were that. No, Sander had something else—something that was a mixture of an aura of power blended with raw male sexuality. She had sensed it as a naive teenager and been drawn to him because of it, and even now, when she was old enough and wise enough to know better, she still felt the pull of his sexual magnetism, its threat to suck her into treacherous waters.

A shiver that was almost a mocking caress stroked over her, making her hug her arms around her body to conceal the sudden unwanted peaking of her nipples. Not because of Sander, she assured herself. No, it was the cold from the open door that was causing her body's sensitive reactions.

Sander's brooding gaze swept over Ruby and rested momentarily on her breasts. Like a leashed cougar, the desire inside him surged against its restraint, leaping and clawing against its imprisonment, the force of its power straining the muscles he had locked against it.

These last couple of weeks he had spent more hours than he wanted to count wrestling with the ache for her that burned in his groin—possessed by it, driven by it, and half maddened by it in equal parts.

No woman had ever been allowed to control him through his desire for her, and for the space of a handful of seconds he was torn—tempted to listen to the inner voice that was warning him to walk away from her, from the desire that had erupted out of nowhere when he had kissed her. A desire like that couldn't be controlled, it could only be appeased. Like some ancient mythical god it demanded sacrifice and self-immolation on its altar.

And then he saw the twins running towards him, and any thought of protecting himself vanished, overwhelmed by the surge of love that flooded him. He hunkered down and held out his arms to them.

Watching the small scene, Ruby felt her throat threaten to close up on a huge lump of emotion. A father with his sons, holding them, protecting them, loving them. There was nothing she would not risk to give her sons that, she acknowledged fiercely.

Holding his sons, Sander knew that there was nothing more important to him than they were— no matter how much he mistrusted their mother.

'Mummy says that we can call you Daddy if we want to.'

That was Freddie, Sander recognised. He had always thought of himself as someone who could control and conceal his emotions, but right now they were definitely threatening to overwhelm him.

'And do you want to?' he asked them, his hold tightening.

'Luke at school has a daddy. He bought him a new bicycle.'

He was being tested, Sander recognised, unable to stop himself from looking towards Ruby.

'Apparently Luke's father also takes him to football matches and to McDonalds.' She managed to answer Sander's unspoken question.

Sander looked at the twins.

'The bicycles are a maybe—once we've found bikes that are the right size for you—and the football is a definite yes. As for McDonalds—well, I think we should leave it to your mother to decide about that.'

Ruby was torn between relief and resentment. Anyone would think he'd been dealing with the twins from birth. He couldn't have given them a better answer if she had scripted it herself.

'Are you ready?' Sander asked Ruby, in the cold, distant voice he always used when he spoke to her.

Ruby looked down at the jeans and loose-fitting sweater she was wearing, the jeans tucked into the boots her sister had given her for Christmas. No doubt Sander was more used to the company of stunning-looking women dressed in designer clothes and jewels—women who had probably spent hours primping and preening themselves to impress him. A small forlorn ache came from nowhere to pierce her heart. Pretty clothes, never mind designer clothes, were a luxury she simply couldn't afford, and they would have been impractical for her life even if she could.

'Yes, we're ready. Boys, go and get your duffel coats,' she instructed, turning back into the hall to get the case she had packed, and almost being knocked over by the twins as they rushed by.

It was Sander's fingers closing round her arm that saved her from stumbling, but the shock of the physical contact with him froze her into immobility, making her feel far more in danger of losing her balance than the twins' dash past her had done.

Her arm felt thin and frail, in direct contrast to the sturdiness of the twins' limbs, he thought. And her face was pinched, as though she didn't always get enough to eat. A question hovered inside his head…an awareness of deprivation that he pushed away from himself.

Although he was standing behind her she could still smell the scent of his cologne, and feel the warmth coming off his body. Inside her head an image formed of the way he had kissed her such a short time ago. Panic and fear clawed at her stomach, adding to her existing tension. She saw Sander's gaze drop to her mouth and her whole body began to tremble.

It would be so easy to give in to the desire clawing at him—so easy to take her as quickly and wantonly as the way she was offering herself to him. His body wanted that. It wanted the heat of her eager muscles wrapped greedily round it, riding his deepening thrusts. It wanted the swift, savage release her body promised.

It might, but did he really want the kind of cheap, tawdry thrill a woman like her peddled— had been peddling the night they had met?

Ruby's small anguished moan as she pulled free of him brought him back to reality.

'Is this your only case?' he demanded, looking away from her to the shabby case on the hall floor.

Ruby nodded her head, and Sander's mouth

twisted with contempt. Of course she would want to underline her poverty to him. Marriage to him was her access to a brand new bank account, filled with money. No doubt she was already planning her first spending spree. He remembered how much delight his mother had always taken in spending his father's money, buying herself couture clothes and expensive jewellery. As a child he'd thought her so beautiful, too dazzled by her glamorous exterior to recognise the corruption that it concealed.

Sander was tempted to ignore the hint Ruby was plainly intending to give him and let her travel to the island with the single shabby case, but that would mean punishing his sons as well as her, he suspected—and besides, he had no wish to make his marriage the subject of speculation and gossip, which it would be if Ruby didn't have a wardrobe commensurate with his own wealth and position.

'Our marriage will take place this Friday,' he told her. 'On Saturday we fly to the island.

You've done as I instructed with regard to the birth control pill, I trust?'

'Yes,' Ruby confirmed.

'Can you prove it?'

Ruby was outraged that he should doubt her, but scorched pride had her fumbling angrily with the clasp of her handbag, both her hands shaking with the force of her emotions as she delved into her bag and produced the foil-backed pack of pills, quite plainly showing the empty spaces from the pills she had already taken.

If she had hoped to shame Sander into an apology she soon recognised that one would not be forthcoming. A curt nod of his head was the only response he seemed willing to give her before he continued cynically,

'And, having fulfilled your obligation, you now expect me to fulfil what you no doubt consider to be mine, I expect? To furnish you with the wherewithal to replace your single suitcase with a full set of new ones and clothes with which to fill them.'

The open cynicism in his voice burned Ruby's already scorched pride like salt poured into an open wound. 'Your only obligation to me is to be a good father to the twins.'

'No,' he corrected her coldly, 'that is my obligation to them.' He didn't like her response. It wasn't the one he had expected. It didn't match the profile he had mentally drawn up for her. Somehow she had managed to stray from the script he had written. The one in which she revealed herself to be an unworthy mother, leaving him holding the high ground and the moral right to continue to despise her. 'There is no need to be self-sacrificing.' Her resistance to the role he had cast for her made him feel all the more determined to prove himself right. 'As my wife, naturally you must present an appropriate appearance—although I must caution you against buying clothes of the type you were wearing the night you propositioned me. It is the role of my wife you will be playing in future. Not the role of a whore.'

Ruby had no words to refute his contemptuous insult, but she wasn't going to accept his charity. 'We already have plenty of clothes. We don't need any more,' she insisted vehemently.

She was daring to try to reject what he knew to be the truth about her. She must be taught a lesson that would ensure that she did not do so again. She *would* wear clothes bought with his money, so that they would both know just what she was. He might be forced to marry her in order to be able to lay legal claim to his sons, but he wasn't going to let her forget that she belonged to that group of women all too willing to sell their bodies to any man rich enough to provide them with the lifestyle of designer clothes and easy money they craved.

'Plenty of clothes?' he taunted her. 'In one case? When there are three of you? My sons and my wife will be dressed in a manner appropriate to their station in life, and not—'

'Not what?' Ruby challenged him.

'Do you *really* need me to answer that question?' was his silkily derisory response.

The shabby case was in the boot of a very expensive and luxurious-looking car, the twins were safely strapped into their seats, her decision had already been made—and yet now that it came to it Ruby wavered on the front doorstep, looking back into the house.

'Where's your coat?'

Sander's question distracted her.

'I don't need one,' she fibbed. The truth was that she didn't have a proper winter coat, but she wasn't going to tell Sander that—not after what he'd already said. He was waiting, holding the car door open for her. Shivering in the easterly March wind, Ruby locked the front door. Her head pounding painfully, she got into the car. Its interior smelled of expensive leather, very different from the smell inside the taxi that had transported them back to Sander's hotel that fateful night…

Her mouth went dry.

The twins were both engrossed in the TVs installed in the back of the front seats. Sander was concentrating on his driving. Now wasn't the time to think about that night, she told herself. But it was too late. The memories were already storming her defences and flooding over them.

Her parents' death in an accident had been a terrible shock, followed by her sister's decision to sell their family home. Ruby hadn't realised then that their parents had died heavily in debt. Her oldest sister had tried to protect her by not telling her, and so she had assumed that her decision to sell the house was motivated by the decision to set up her own interior design business in Cheshire. Angry with her sister, she had deliberately chosen to befriend a girl new to the area, knowing that her sister disapproved of the freedom Tracy's parents allowed her, and of Tracy herself. Although she was only eighteen months older than Ruby, Tracy had been far more worldly, dressing in tight-fitting clothes in the latest and skimpiest fashions, her hair dyed blonde and her face heavily made-up.

Secretly, although she hadn't been prepared to admit it—especially not to her older sister— Ruby had been shocked by some of the disclosures Tracy had made about the things she had done. Tracy's goal in life was to get a footballer boyfriend. She had heard that young footballers in Manchester patronised a certain club in the city, and had asked Ruby to go there with her.

Alarmed by Tracy's disclosures, Ruby hadn't really wanted to go. But when she had tried to say so, telling Tracy that she doubted her sister would give her permission, Tracy had mocked her and accused her of being a baby who needed her sister's permission for everything she did. Of course Ruby had denied that she was any such thing, whereupon Tracy had challenged her to prove it by daring her to go with her.

She had been just seventeen, and a very naive seventeen at that, with her whole world turned upside down by events over which she'd had no control. But no matter how often both her sisters had reassured her since then that her rebellion had been completely natural, understandable, and that she was not to blame for what had happened, Ruby knew that deep down inside she would always feel guilty.

Before they'd left for Manchester Tracy had promised Ruby a 'makeover' and poured them both a glass of vodka and orange juice. It had gone straight to Ruby's head as she had never drunk alcohol. The drink had left her feeling so light-headed that she hadn't protested or objected when Tracy had insisted that Ruby change into one of her own short skirts and a tight-fitting top, before making up Ruby's face in a similar style to her own, with dark eyeliner, heavy thick mascara loaded on her eyelashes and lots of deep pink lipgloss.

The girl staring back at Ruby from the mirror, with her tousled hair and her pink pout had been so unrecognisable as herself that under the effect of the vodka and orange Ruby had only been able to stare at her reflection in dizzy astonishment.

She might only have been seventeen, but she had known even before she had watched Tracy sweet talking the bouncer into letting them into the club that neither her parents nor her sisters would have approved of her being there, but by then she had been too afraid of Tracy's mockery and contempt to tell her that she had changed her mind and wanted to go home.

She'd watched other girls going in—older girls than her, dressed up to the nines in tiny little tops and skirts that revealed dark sunbed tans—and she'd known instinctively and immediately that she would feel out of place.

Inside, the club had been hot and stuffy, packed with girls with the same goal in mind as Tracy.

Several young men had come up to them as they'd stood close to the bar. Tracy had refused Ruby's suggestion that they sit down at a tucked-away table with a derisory, 'Don't be daft—no one will see us if we do that.' But

Tracy had shaken her head, ignoring the boys and telling Ruby, 'They're nothing. Just ordinary lads out on the pull.'

She'd bought them both drinks—cocktails which had seemed innocuous when Ruby sipped thirstily at hers, because of the heat in the club, but which had quickly made her feel even more dizzy and disorientated than the vodka and orange juice had done.

The club had been packed and noisy, and Ruby's head had begun to ache. She had felt alien and alone, with the alcohol heightening her emotions: bringing home to her the reality of her parents' death, bringing to a head all the despair and misery she had been feeling.

Tracy had started talking to a young man, deliberately excluding Ruby from their conversation and keeping her back to her.

Suddenly and achingly Ruby had longed for the security of the home life she had lost—of knowing that there was someone in her life to take care of her and protect her, someone who loved her, instead of getting cross with her like her elder sister did. And that had been when she had looked across the bar and seen Sander.

Something about him had set him apart from the other men in the bar. For a start he'd been far more smartly dressed, in a suit, with his dark hair groomed, and an air of command and power and certainty had emanated from him that Ruby's insecure senses immediately recognised and were drawn to… In her alcohol-induced state, Sander had looked like an island of security and safety in a sea of confusion and misery. She hadn't been able to take her eyes off him, and when he had looked back at her, her mouth had gone so dry with the anticipation of speaking to him that she had had to wet her lips with the tip of her tongue. The way that Sander's gaze had followed that movement, showing her that he was singling her out from all the other girls in the bar, had reinforced Ruby's cocktail-produced belief that there was a link between them—that he was drawing her to him, that they were meant to meet, and that somehow once she was close to him she would be safe, and he would save her from her own fears and protect her just as her parents had done.

She had no memory of actually going to him, only of reaching him, feeling like a swimmer who had crested turbulent waves to reach the security of a calm sea where she could float safely. When she had smiled up at Sander she had felt as though she already knew him. But of course she hadn't. She hadn't known anything, Ruby reflected bitterly now, as she dragged her thoughts away from the past and massaged her throbbing temple as Sander drove onto the motorway slip road and the car picked up speed.

CHAPTER FOUR

SANDER had booked them into the Carlton Towers Hotel, just off Sloane Street. They had an enormous suite of three bedrooms, each with its own bathroom, and a good-sized sitting room as well.

Ruby had felt dreadfully out of place as they'd walked through the downstairs lobby, compared with the elegantly groomed women surrounded by expensive-looking shopping bags who were having afternoon tea in the lounge. But she had soon forgotten them once they had been shown into their suite and she had realised that Sander would be staying in the suite with them.

Her heart was beating far too fast, her whole body suddenly charged and sensitised, so that she was far too aware of Sander. His presence in the room, even though there were several feet between them and he was fully dressed, somehow had the same effect on her body as though he was standing close to her and touching her. The sound of his voice made her think she could almost feel the warmth of his breath on her skin. Her body was starting to react even to her thoughts, tiny darts of sensation heightening her awareness of him.

He raised his hand, gesturing towards the bedrooms as he told her, 'I've asked for one of the rooms to be made up with twin beds for the boys.'

Inside her head she could feel that hand cupping her breast. Beneath her clothes her breasts swelled and ached whilst she tried desperately to stifle her body's arousal. Why was this happening to her? She'd lived happily without sex for nearly six years. Why was her body reacting like this now?

It was just reacting to memory, that was all. Her desire for Sander, like that memory, belonged to the past and had no place in the present. Ruby tried to convince herself, but she knew that it wasn't true. The fact that he could arouse her to intense desire for him was something she didn't want to think about. Her stomach was churning, adding to the feeling of nausea already being produced by her headache. She had actually been sick when they had stopped for a break at a motorway service station, and had had to purchase a travel pack of toothbrush and toothpaste to refresh her mouth. Now all she really wanted to do was lie down in a dark room, but of course that was impossible.

'You and I will occupy the other two rooms, of course,' Sander was saying. 'I expect that you will wish to have the room closest to the boys?'

'I could have shared a room with them,' was Ruby's response. Because sharing with the boys would surely prevent any more of those unwanted memories from surfacing? 'There was no need for you to book three rooms.'

'If I had only booked two the hotel would have

assumed you would be sharing my bed, not sleeping with the twins,' was Sander's response.

Immediately another image flashed through her head: two naked bodies entwined on a large bed, the man's hands holding and caressing the woman, whilst her head was thrown back in wild ecstasy. Sander's hands and her head. Heat filled her body. Her own mental images were making her panic. What she was experiencing was probably caused by the same kind of thing that caused the victims of dreadful trauma to have flashbacks they couldn't control, she told herself. They meant nothing other than that Sander's un-expected and unwanted reappearance in her life was causing her to remember the event that had had such a dramatic effect on her life.

To her relief the twins, who had been inspect-ing the suite, came rushing into the sitting room. Harry ran over to her to inform her, 'Guess what? There's a TV in our bedroom, and—'

'A TV which will remain switched off whilst you are in bed,' Ruby told him firmly, relieved to be able to return to the familiar role of motherhood. 'You know the rules.' She was very strict about limiting the boys' television viewing, preferring them to make their own entertainment.

Sander's comment about the rooms had penetrated her mind and was still lodged there—a small, unnerving time bomb of a comment that was having an effect on her that was out of all proportion to its reality. The sound of Sander saying 'my bed' had made her heart jerk around inside her chest as though it was on a string—and why? She had no desire to share that bed with him; he meant nothing to her now. It was merely the result of only ever having had one sexual partner and being sexually inexperienced. It had left her reacting to a man saying the words 'my bed' as though she were a teenager, blushing at every mention of anything remotely connected to sex, Ruby derided herself.

'I thought we'd use the rest of the afternoon to get the boys kitted out with the clothes they'll need for the island. We can walk to Harrods from here, or get a cab if you wish.'

The last thing Ruby felt like doing was shopping, but she was determined not to show any weakness. Sander would only accuse of being a bad mother if she did.

Hopefully she might see a chemist, where she could get something for her headache. It had been so long since she had last had one of these debilitating attacks that she didn't have anything she could take for it. Determinedly trying to ignore her continuing feeling of nausea, she nodded her head, and then winced as the pain increased.

'The boys will need summer clothes,' Sander told her. 'Even in March the temperature on the island can be as high as twenty-two degrees centigrade, and it rises to well over thirty in the summer.'

Two hours later Ruby was battling between angry frustration at the way in which Sander had overruled all her attempts to minimise the amount of money he was spending by choosing the cheapest items she could find and a mother's natural pride in her sons, who had drawn smiles of approval from the assistants with their appearance in their new clothes: smart, boyish separates from the summer ranges that had just come in, and in which Ruby had to admit they looked adorable.

As a reward for their good behaviour Sander had insisted on taking them to the toy department, where he'd bought them both complicated-looking state-of-the-art boys' toys that had them both speechless with delight.

The whole time they had been shopping with the boys Ruby had been conscious of the admiring looks Sander had attracted from other women—women who no doubt would have been only too delighted to be marrying him in two days' time, Ruby acknowledged, and her heart gave a flurry of tense beats in response to her thoughts.

'I've got some business matters to attend to this evening,' Sander told her as they made a detour on the way back to the hotel to allow the boys to walk in Hyde Park—a suggestion from Sander which Ruby had welcomed, hoping that the fresh air would ease the pounding in her head.

After acknowledging Sander's comment Ruby focused on keeping an eye on the twins, who were walking ahead of them.

Sander continued. 'But first I've arranged for a jeweller to come to the hotel with a selection of wedding and engagement rings. I've also made an appointment for you tomorrow morning at the spa and hair salon in Harvey Nichols, and then afterwards a personal shopper will help you choose your own new wardrobe. I thought I'd take the boys to the Natural History Museum whilst you're doing that, to keep them occupied.'

Ruby stopped walking and turned to look at him, her eyes blazing with temper.

'I don't need a spa appointment, or a new

hairstyle, or a new wardrobe, thank you very much. And I certainly don't want an engagement ring.'

She was lying, of course. Or did she think she could get more out of him by pretending she didn't want anything?

Oblivious to Sander's thoughts, Ruby continued, 'And if my present appearance isn't good enough for you, then too bad. Because it's good enough for me.'

Quickly hurrying after the twins, Ruby tried to ignore how unwell she was feeling. Even though she couldn't see him she knew that Sander had caught up with her and was standing behind her. Her body could feel him there, but stubbornly she refused to turn round.

'You have two choices,' Sander informed her coolly. 'Either you accept the arrangements I have made for you, or you will accept the clothes I shall instruct the store to select on your behalf. There is no option for you, as my wife, to dress as you are doing now. You are so eager to display your body to male eyes that you aren't even wearing a coat—all the better for them to assess what is on offer, no doubt.'

'That's a disgusting thing to say, and totally untrue. You must *know* the reason I'm not wearing a coat is—' Abruptly Ruby stopped speaking realising that she had allowed her anger to betray her into making an admission she had no wish to make.

'Yes?' Sander probed.

'Is that I forgot to bring one with me,' Ruby told him lamely. The truth was that she had not been able to afford to buy herself one—not with the twins constantly outgrowing their clothes. But she wasn't going to expose herself to more humiliation by admitting that to Sander.

How could he be marrying a woman like this one? Sander wondered savagely. It would have suited his purposes far more if the report he had received from the agents he had hired to find Ruby had included something to suggest that she was a neglectful mother, thus giving him real grounds for legally removing them from their mother. The report, though, had done nothing of the sort—had actually dared to claim that Ruby was a good mother, the kind of mother whose absence from their lives would damage his sons. That was a risk he was not prepared to take.

Ignoring Ruby's defiant statement, Sander went on, 'The boys are approaching an age where they will be aware of appearance and other people's opinions. They are going to have to deal with settling into a different environment, and I'm sure that the last thing you want to do is make it harder for them. I have a duty to the Konstantinakos position as the ruling and thus most important family on the island. That duty involves a certain amount of entertaining. It will be expected that as my wife you take part in that. Additionally, my sister, her friends, and the wives of those of my executives who live in Athens are very fashion-conscious. They would be quick to sense that our marriage is not all it should be were you to make a point of dressing as you do now. And that could impact on our sons.'

Our sons. Ruby felt as though her heart had been squeezed by a giant hand. She was very tempted to resort to the immature tactic of pointing out that since he hadn't even been aware of the twins' existence until recently he was hardly in a position to take a stance on delivering advice to her on what might or might not affect them—but what was the point? He had won—again, she was forced to acknowledge. Because now she would be very conscious of the fact that she was being judged by her appearance, and that if she was found wanting it would reflect on the twins. Acceptance by their peers was very important to children. Ruby knew that even at the boys' young age children hated being 'different' or being embarrassed. For their sake she would have to accept Sander's charity, even though her pride hated the idea.

She hated feeling so helpless and dependent on others. She loved her sisters, and was infinitely grateful to them for all that they had done for her and the boys, but it was hard sometimes always having to depend on others, never being able to claim the pride and self-respect that came from being financially self-supporting. She had hoped that once the boys were properly settled at school she might be able to earn a degree that ultimately would allow her to find work, but now she was going to be even more dependent on the financial generosity of someone else than she was already. But it wasn't her pride that was important, Ruby reminded herself. It was her sons' emotional happiness. They hadn't asked to be born. And she hadn't asked for Sander's opinion on her appearance—or his money. She was twenty-three, and it was ridiculous of her to feel so helpless and humiliated that she was close to defeated tears.

To conceal her emotions she leaned down

towards the boys, to warn them not to run too far ahead of them, watching as they nodded their heads.

It was when she straightened up that it happened. Perhaps she moved too quickly. Ruby didn't know, but one minute she was straightening up and the next she felt so dizzy from the pain in her head that she lost her balance. She would have fallen if Sander hadn't reacted so quickly, reaching out to grab hold of her so that she fell against his body rather than tumbling to the ground.

Immediately she was transported back to the past. The circumstances might be very different, but then too she had stumbled, and Sander had rescued her. Then, though, the cause of her fall had been the unfamiliar height of the borrowed shoes Tracy had insisted she should wear, and the effect of too many cocktails. The result was very much the same. Now, just as then, she could feel the steady thud of Sander's heart against her body, whilst her own raced and bounced, the frantic speed of its beat making her feel breathless and far too weak to try to struggle against the arms holding her. Then too his proximity had filled her senses with the scent of his skin, the alien maleness of hard muscle beneath warm flesh, the power of that maleness, both physically and emotionally, and most of all her own need to simply be held by him. Then she had been thrilled to be in his arms, but now… Panic curled through her. That was not how she was supposed to feel, and it certainly wasn't what she wanted to feel. Sander was her enemy—an enemy she was forced to share her sons with because he was their father, an enemy who had ripped from her the protection of her naivety with his cruel contempt for her.

Determinedly Ruby started to push herself free, but instead of releasing her Sander tightened his hold of her.

He'd seen that she was slender, Sander acknowledged, but it was only now that he was holding her and could actually feel the bones beneath her flesh that he was able to recognise how thin she was. She was shivering too, despite her claim not to need a coat. Once again he was reminded of the report he had commissioned on her. Was it possible that in order to ensure that her sons ate well and were not deprived of the nourishment they needed she herself had been going without? Sander had held his sons, and he knew just how solid and strong their bodies were. The amount of energy they possessed alone was testament to their good health. And it was *their* good health that mattered to him, not that of their mother, whose presence in his life as well as theirs was something he had told himself he would have to accept for their sakes.

Even so… He looked down into Ruby's face. Her skin was paler than he remembered, but he had put that down to the fact that when he had first met her her face had been plastered in make-up, whilst now she wore none. Her cheekbones might be more pronounced, but her lips were still full and soft—the lips of sensual siren who knew just how to use her body to her own advantage. Sander had never been under any illusions as to why Ruby had approached him. He had heard her and her friend discussing the rich footballers they intended to target. Unable to find one, Ruby had obviously decided to target him instead.

Sander frowned, unwilling to contrast the frail vulnerability of the woman he was holding with the girl he remembered, and even more unwilling to allow himself to feel concern for her. Why should he care about her? He didn't. And yet as she struggled to pull free of him, her eyes huge in her fine boned face, a sudden gleam of March sunshine pierced the heavy grey of the late afternoon sky to reveal the perfection of her skin and stroke fingers of light through her blonde curls, Sander had sudden reluctance to let her go. In rejection of it he immediately released her.

It was the unexpected swiftness of her release after Sander's grip had seemed to be tightening on her that was causing her to feel so…confused, Ruby told herself, refusing to allow herself to use the betraying word *bereft*, which had tried to slip through her defences. Why should she feel bereft? She wanted to be free. Sander's hold had no appeal for her. She certainly hadn't spent the last six years longing to be back in his arms. Why should she, when her last memory of them had been the biting pressure of his fingers in her flesh as he thrust her away from him in a gesture of angry contempt?

It had started to rain, causing Ruby to shiver and call the boys to them. It was no good her longing for the security of home, she told herself as they headed back to the hotel in the taxi Sander had flagged down, with the twins squashed in between them so that she didn't have to come into contact with him. She must focus on the future and all that it would hold for her sons. Their happiness was far more important to her than her own, and it was obvious to her how easily they were adapting to Sander's presence in their lives. An acceptance oiled by the promise of expensive toys, Ruby thought bitterly, knowing that her sons were too young for her to be able to explain to them that a parent's love wasn't always best shown though gifts and treats, and knowing too that it would be part of her future role to ensure that they were not spoiled by their father's wealth or blinded to the reality of other people's lives and struggles.

Once they were back in their suite, in the privacy of her bathroom, Ruby tried to take two of the painkiller tablets she had bought from the chemist's she had gone into on the pretext of needing some toothpaste. But her stomach heaved at the mere thought of attempting to swallow them, nausea overwhelming her.

Still feeling sick, and weakened by her pounding headache, as soon as the twins had

had something to eat she bathed them and put them to bed.

They had only been asleep a few minutes when the jeweller Sander had summoned arrived, removing a roll of cloth from his brief-case, after Sander had introduced him to Ruby and they had all sat down.

Placing the roll on the class coffee table, he unfolded it—and Ruby had to suppress a gasp of shock when she saw the glitter of the rings inside it.

They were all beautiful, but something made Ruby recoil from them. It seemed somehow shabby and wrong to think of wearing some-thing so precious. A ring should represent love and commitment that were equally precious and enduring instead of the hollow emptiness her marriage would be.

'You choose,' she told Sander emptily, not wanting to look at them.

Her lack of interest in the priceless gems glit-tering in front of her made Sander frown. His mother had loved jewellery. He could see her now, seated at her dressing table, dressed to go out for the evening, admiring the antique Cartier bangles glittering on her arms.

'Your birth paid for these,' she had told him. 'Your grandfather insisted that your father should only buy me one, so I had to remind him that I had given birth to his heir. Thank goodness you weren't a girl. Your grandfather is so mean that he would have seen to it that I got nothing if you had been. Remember when you are a man, Sander, that the more expensive the piece of jewellery you give a woman, the more willing she will be, and thus the more you can demand of her.' She had laughed then, pouting her glossy red lipsticked lips at her own reflection and adding, 'I shouldn't really give away the secrets of my sex to you, should I?'

His beautiful, shallow, greedy mother—chosen as a bride for his father by his grandfather because of her aristocratic Greek ancestry, marrying his father because she hated her own family's poverty. When he had grown old enough to recognise the way in which his gentle academic father had been humiliated and treated with contempt by the father who had forced the marriage on him, and the wife who thought of him only as an open bank account, Sander had sworn he would never follow in his father's footsteps and allow the same thing to happen to him.

What was Ruby hoping for by pretending a lack of interest? Something more expensive? Angrily Sander looked at the rings, his hand hovering over the smallest solitaire he could see. His intention was to punish her by choosing it for her—until his attention was drawn to another ring close to it, its two perfect diamonds shimmering in the light.

Feeling too ill to care what kind of engagement ring she had, Ruby exhaled in relief when she saw Sander select one of the rings. All she wanted was for the whole distasteful charade to be over.

'We'll have this one,' Sander told the jeweller

abruptly, his voice harsh with the irritation he felt against himself for his own sentimentality.

It was the jeweller who handed the ring to Ruby, not Sander. She took it unwillingly, sliding the cold metal onto her finger, her eyes widening and her heart turning over inside her chest as she looked at it properly for the first time. Two perfect diamonds nestled together on a slender band, slightly offset from one another and yet touching—twin diamonds for their twin sons. Her throat closed up, her gaze seeking Sander's despite her attempt to stop it doing so, her emotions clearly on display. But there was no answering warmth in Sander's eyes, only a cold hardness that froze her out.

'An excellent choice,' the jeweller was saying. 'Each stone weighs two carets, and they are a particularly good quality. And of course ethically mined, just as you requested,' he informed Sander.

His comment took Ruby by surprise. From what she knew of Sander she wouldn't have thought it would matter to him *how* the diamonds had been mined, but obviously it did. Meaning what? That she had misjudged him? Meaning nothing, Ruby told herself fiercely. She didn't want to revisit her opinion of Sander, never mind re-evaluate it. Why not? Because she was afraid that if she did so, if she allowed herself to see him in a different light, then she might become even more vulnerable to him than she already was? Emotionally vulnerable as well as sexually vulnerable? No, that must not happen.

Her panic increased her existing nausea, and it was a relief when the jeweller finally left. His departure was quickly followed by Sander's, to his business meeting.

Finally she could give in to her need to go and lie down—after she had checked on the twins, of course.

CHAPTER FIVE

'YOUR hair is lovely and thick, but since it is so curly I think it would look better if we put a few different lengths into it.' Those had been the words of the salon's senior stylist when he had first come over to examine Ruby's hair. She had simply nodded her head, not really caring how he cut her hair. She was still feeling unwell, her head still aching, and she knew from experience that these headaches could last for two and even three days once they took hold, before finally lifting.

Now, though, as the stylist stepped back from the mirror and asked, 'What do you think?' Ruby was forced to admit that she was almost lost for words over the difference his skill had made to her hair, transforming it from an untidy tumble of curls into a stunningly chic style that feathered against her face and swung softly onto her shoulders—the kind of style she had seen worn by several of the women taking tea at the hotel the previous afternoon, a deceptively simple style that breathed expense and elegance.

'I…I love it,' she admitted wanly.

'It's easy to maintain and will fall back into shape after you've washed it. You're lucky to have naturally blonde hair.'

Thanking him, Ruby allowed herself to be led away. At least she had managed to eat some dry toast this morning, and keep down a couple of the painkillers which had eased her head a little, thankfully.

Her next appointment was at the beauty spa, and when she caught other women giving her a second look as she made her way there she guessed that they must be querying the elegance of her new hairstyle set against the shabbiness of her clothes and her make-up-free face.

She hated admitting it, but it *was* true that first

impressions counted, and that people—especially women—judged members of their own sex by their appearance. The last thing she wanted was for the twins to be embarrassed by a mother other women looked down on. Even young children were very perceptive and quick to notice such things.

The spa and beauty salon was ahead of her. Taking a deep breath, Ruby held her head high as she walked in.

Two hours later, when she walked out again with the personal shopper who had come to collect her and help her choose a new wardrobe, Ruby couldn't help giving quick, disbelieving glances into the mirrors she passed, still unable to totally believe that the young woman looking back at her really was her. Her nails were manicured and painted a fashionable dark shade, her eyebrows were trimmed, and her make-up was applied in such a subtle and delicate way that it barely looked as though she was wearing any at all. Yet at the same time her eyes looked larger and darker, her mouth fuller and softer, and her complexion so delicately perfect that Ruby couldn't take her eyes off the glowing face looking back at her. Although she would never admit it to Sander, her makeover had been fun once she had got over her initial discomfort at being fussed over and pampered. Now she felt like a young woman rather than an anxious mother.

'I understand you want clothes suitable for living on a Greek island, rather than merely holidaying there, and that your life there will include various social and business engagements?' Without waiting for Ruby's answer the personal shopper continued. 'Fortunately we have got some of our new season stock in as well as several designers' cruise collections, so I'm sure we shall be able to find everything you need. As for your wedding dress…'

Ruby's heart leapt inside her chest. Somehow

she hadn't expected Sander to specify that she needed a wedding dress.

'It's just a very quiet registry office ceremony,' she told the personal shopper.

'But her wedding day and what she wore when she married the man she loves is still something that a woman always remembers,' the other woman insisted.

The personal shopper was only thinking of the store's profit, Ruby reminded herself. There was no real reason for her to have such an emotional reaction to the words. After all, she didn't love Sander and he certainly didn't love her. What she wore was immaterial, since neither of them was likely to want to look back in future years to remember the day they married. Her thoughts had produced a hard painful lump in her throat and an unwanted ache inside her chest. Why? She was twenty-three years old and the mother of five-year-old sons. She had long ago abandoned any thoughts of romance and love and all that went with those things, dismissing them as the emotional equivalent of choco-late—sweet on the tongue for a very short time, highly addictive and dangerously habit-forming. Best avoided in favour of a sensible and sustaining emotional diet. Like the love she had for her sons and the bond she shared with her sisters. Those were emotions and commitments that would last for a lifetime, whilst from what she had seen and heard romantic love was a delusion.

The twins were fascinated by the exhibits in the Natural History Museum. They had happily held Sander's hand and pressed grati-fyingly close to him for protection, calling him Daddy and showing every indication of being happy to be with him, so why did he feel so aware of Ruby's absence, somehow incom-plete? It was for the boys' sake, Sander assured himself, because he was concerned that they might be missing their mother, nothing more.

* * *

Without quite knowing how it had happened, Ruby had acquired a far more extensive and expensive wardrobe than she had wanted. Every time she had protested or objected the personal shopper had overruled her—politely and pleasantly, but nonetheless determinedly— insisting that her instructions were that Ruby must have a complete wardrobe that would cover a wide variety of situations. And of course the clothes were sinfully gorgeous—beautifully cut trousers and shorts in cream linen, with a matching waistcoat lined in the same silk as the unstructured shirt that went with them, soft flowing silk dresses, silk and cotton tops, formal fitted cocktail dresses, along with more casual but still frighteningly expensive 'leisure and beach clothes', as the personal shopper had described them. There were also shoes for every occasion and each outfit, and underwear— scraps of silk and lace that Ruby had wanted to reject in favour of something far more sensible, but which somehow or other had been added to the growing rail of clothes described by the personal shopper as 'must-haves'.

Now all that was left was the wedding dress, and the personal shopper was producing with a flourish a cream dress with a matching jacket telling Ruby proudly, 'Vera Wang, from her new collection. Since the dress is short and beautifully tailored it is ideal for a registry office wedding, and of course you could wear it afterwards as a cocktail dress. It was actually ordered by another customer, but unfortunately when it came it was too small for her. I'm sure that it will fit you, and the way the fabric is pleated will suit your body shape.'

What she meant was that the waterfall of pleated ruching that was a feature of the cream silk-satin dress would disguise how thin she was, Ruby suspected.

The dress was beautiful, elegant and feminine, and exactly the kind of dress that a woman would remember wearing on her wedding day—which was exactly why she didn't want to wear it. But the dresser was waiting expectantly.

It fitted her perfectly. Cut by a master hand, it shaped her body in a way that made her waist appear far narrower surely than it actually was, whilst somehow adding a feminine curvaceousness to her shape that made Ruby think she was looking at someone else in the mirror and not herself: the someone else she might have been if things had been different. If Sander had loved her?

Shakily Ruby shook her head and started to take the dress off, desperate to escape from the cruel reality of the image the mirror had thrown back at her. She could never be the woman she had seen in the mirror—a woman so loved by her man that she had the right to claim everything the dress offered her and promised him.

'No. I don't want it,' she told the bewildered-looking personal shopper. 'Please take it away. I'll wear something else.'

'But it was perfect on you…'

Still Ruby shook her head.

She was in the changing room getting dressed when the personal shopper reappeared, carrying a warm-looking, casually styled off-white parka.

'I nearly forgot,' she told Ruby, 'your husband-to-be said that you had left your coat at home by accident and that you needed something warm to wear whilst you are in London.'

Wordlessly Ruby took the parka from her. It was lined with soft checked wool, and well-made as well as stylish.

'It's a new designer,' the shopper told her. 'And a line that we're just trialling. She's Italian, trained by Prada.'

Ruby bent her head so that the personal shopper wouldn't see the emotion sheening her eyes. Sander might have protected her in public by pretending to believe that she had forgotten her coat, but in private he had humiliated her—because Ruby knew that he had guessed that she didn't really possess a winter coat, and that she had been shivering with cold yesterday when they had walked in the park.

Walking back to the hotel wrapped in her new parka, Ruby reflected miserably that beneath the new hairstyle and the pretty make-up she was still exactly what she had been before-hand—they couldn't change her, could not take away the burden of the guilt she still carried because of what she had once been. Expensive clothes were only a pretence—just like her marriage to Sander would be.

For her. Yes, but not for the twins. They must never know how she felt. The last thing she wanted was for them to grow up feeling that she had sacrificed herself for them. They must believe that she was happy.

She had intended to go straight to the suite, but the assessing look a woman in the lobby gave her, before smiling slightly to herself, as though she was satisfied that Ruby couldn't compete with her, stung her pride enough to have her changing her mind and heading for the lounge instead.

A well-trained waitress showed her to a small table right at the front of the lounge. Ruby would have preferred to have hidden herself away in a dark corner, her brief surge of defiance having retreated leaving her feeling self-conscious and very alone. She wasn't used to being on her own. Normally when she went out she had the twins with her, or one of her sisters.

When the waitress came to take her order Ruby asked for tea. She hadn't eaten anything all day but she wasn't hungry. She was too on edge for that.

The lounge was filling up. Several very smart-looking women were coming in, followed by a group of businessmen in suits, one of whom gave her such a deliberate look followed by a warm smile that Ruby felt her face beginning to burn.

She was just about to pour herself a cup of tea when she saw the twins hurrying towards her followed by Sander. His hair, like the twins', was damp, as though he had just stepped out of the shower. Her heart lurched into her ribs. Her hand had started to tremble so badly that she had to put down the teapot. The twins were clamouring to tell her about their day, but even though she tried desperately to focus on them her gaze remained riveted to Sander, who had now stopped walking and was looking at her.

It wasn't her changed appearance that had brought him to an abrupt halt, though.

In Sander's eyes the new hairstyle and pretty make-up were merely window-dressing that highlighted what he already knew and what had been confirmed to him when Ruby had opened the door of her home to him a few days earlier—namely that the delicacy of her features possessed a rare beauty.

No, what had caused him to stop dead almost in mid-stride was the sense of male pride the sight of the trio in front of him brought. His sons and their mother. Not just his sons, but the *three* of them. They went together, belonged together—belonged to him? Sander shook his head, trying to dispel his atavistic and unfamiliar reactions with regard to Ruby, both angered by them and wanting to reject them. They were so astonishingly the opposite of what he wanted to feel. What was happening to him?

Her transformation passed him by other than the fact that he noticed the way she was wearing her hair revealed the slender column of her throat and that her face had a bit more colour in it.

Ruby, already self-conscious about the changes to her appearance, held her breath, waiting for Sander to make some comment. After all the sight of her had brought him to a halt. But when he reached the table he simply frowned and demanded to know why she hadn't ordered something to eat.

'Because all I wanted was a cup of tea,' she answered him. Didn't he like her new haircut? Was that why he was looking so grim? Well, she certainly wasn't going to ask him if he approved of the change. She turned to the boys, asking them, 'Did you like the Natural History Museum?'

'Yes,' Harry confirmed. 'And then Daddy took us swimming.'

Swimming? Ruby directed a concerned look at Sander.

'There's a pool here in the hotel,' he explained. 'Since the boys will be living on an island, I wanted to make sure that they can swim.'

'Daddy bought us new swimming trunks,' Freddie told her.

'There should be two adults with them when they go in a pool,' Ruby couldn't stop herself from saying. 'A child can drown in seconds and—'

'There was a lifeguard on duty.' Sander stopped her. 'They're both naturals in the water, but that will be in their genes. My brother swam for Greece as a junior.'

'Mummy's hair is different,' Harry suddenly announced.

Self-consciousness crawled along her spine. Now surely Sander must say something about her transformation, give at least some hint of approval since he was the one who had orchestrated her makeover, but instead he merely stated almost indifferently, 'I hope you got everything you are going to need, as there won't be time for any more shopping. As I said, I've arranged for us to fly to the island the day after the marriage ceremony.'

Ruby nodded her head. It was silly of her to feel disappointed because Sander hadn't said anything about her new look. Silly or dangerous? His approval or lack of it shouldn't mean anything to her at all.

The boys would be hungry, and she was tired. She was their mother, though, and it was far more important that she focused on her maternal responsibilities rather than worrying about Sander's approval or lack of it.

'I'll take the boys up to the suite and organise a meal for them,' she told Sander.

'Good idea. I've got some ends to tie up with the Embassy,' he said brusquely, with a brief nod of his head.

'What about dinner?' Ruby's mouth had gone dry, and the silence that greeted her question made her feel she had committed as much of a *faux pas* as if she'd asked him to go to bed with her.

Feeling hot and angry with herself for inadvertently giving Sander the impression that she wanted to have dinner with him, she swallowed against the dry feeling in her mouth.

Why had Ruby's simple question brought back that atavistic feeling he had had earlier? Sander asked himself angrily. For a moment he let himself imagine the two of them having dinner together. The two of them? Surely he meant the four of them—for it was because of the twins and only because of them that he had decided to allow her back into his life. Sander knew better than to allow himself to be tricked by female emotions, be they maternal or sexual. As he had good cause to know, those emotions could be summoned out of nowhere and disappear back there just as quickly.

'I've already arranged to have dinner with an old friend,' he lied. 'I don't know what time I'll be back.'

An old friend, Sander had said. Did that mean he was having dinner with another woman? A lover, perhaps? Ruby wondered later, after the boys had eaten their tea and she had forced herself to eat something with them. She knew so little about Sander's life and the people in it. A feeling of panic began to grow inside her.

'Mummy, come and look at our island,' Freddie was demanding, standing in front of a laptop that he was trying to open.

'No, Freddie, you mustn't touch that,' Ruby protested,

'It's all right, Mummy,' Harry assured her

adopting a heartbreakingly familiar pose of male confidence. 'Daddy said that we could look.'

Freddie had got the laptop lid up—like all children, the twins were very at home with modern technology—and before Ruby could say anything the screen was filled with the image of an almost crescent shaped island, with what looked like a range of rugged mountains running the full length of its spine.

In the early days, after she had first met him, Ruby had tried to find out as much as she could about Sander, still refusing to believe then that all she had been to him was a one-night stand.

She had learned that the island, whose closest neighbour was Cyprus, had been invaded and conquered many times, and that in Sander's veins ran the ruling blood of conquering Moors from the time of the Crusades—even though now the island population considered itself to be Greek. She had also learned that Sander's family had ruled the island for many centuries, and that his grandfather, the current patriarch, had built up a shipping business in the wake of the Second World War which had brought new wealth and employment to the island. However, once she had been forced to recognise that she meant nothing to Sander she had stopped seeking out information about him.

'Bath time,' she told her sons firmly.

Their new clothes and her own had been delivered whilst they had been downstairs, along with some very smart new cases, and once the twins were in bed she intended to spend her evening packing in readiness for their flight to the island.

Only once the boys were bathed and in bed Ruby was drawn back to the computer, with its tantalising image of the island.

Almost without realising what she was doing she clicked on the small red dot that represented its capital. Several thumbnail images immediately appeared. Ruby clicked on the first of them to enlarge it, and revealed a dazzlingly white fortress, perched high on a cliff above an impossibly blue green sea, its Moorish-looking towers reaching up into a deep blue sky. Another thumbnail enlarged to show what she assumed was the front of the same building, looking more classically Greek in design and dominating a formal square. The royal blue of the traditionally dressed guards' jackets worn over brilliantly white skirts made a striking image.

The other images revealed a hauntingly beautiful landscape of sandy bays backed by cliffs, small fishing harbours, and white-capped mountains covered in wild flowers. These were contrasted by a modern cargo dock complex, and small towns of bright white buildings and dark shadowed alleyways. It was impossible not to be captivated by the images of the island, Ruby admitted, but at the same time viewing them had brought home to her how different and even alien the island was to everything she and the twins knew. Was she doing the right thing? She knew nothing of Sander's family, or his way of life, and once on the island she would be totally at his mercy. But if she hadn't agreed to go with them he would have tried to take the twins from her, she was sure. This way at least she would be with them.

A fierce tide of maternal love surged through her. The twins meant everything to her. Their emotional security both now and in the future was what would bring her happiness, and was far more important to her than anything else—especially the unwanted and humiliating desire that Sander was somehow able to arouse in her. Her mouth had gone dry again. At seventeen she might have been able to excuse herself for being vulnerable to Sander's sexual charisma, but she was not seventeen any more. Even if her single solitary memory of sexual passion was still limited to what she had experienced with Sander. He, of course, had no doubt shared his bed with an unending parade of women since he had ejected her so cruelly from both it and his life.

She looked at the computer, suddenly unable

to resist the temptation to do a web search on Sander's name. It wasn't prying, not really. She had the boys to think of after all.

She wasn't sure what she had expected to find, but her eyes widened over the discovery that Sander was now ruler of the island—a role that carried the title of King, although, according to the website, he had decided to dispense with its usage, preferring to adopt a more democratic approach to ruling the island than that exercised by his predecessors.

Apparently his parents had died when Sander was eighteen, in a flying accident. The plane they'd been in piloted by a cousin of Sander's mother. A shock as though she had inadvertently touched a live wire shot through her. They had both been orphaned at almost the same age. Like hers, Sander's parents had been killed in an accident. If she had known that when they had first met… What difference would it have made? None.

Sander was thirty-four, to her twenty-three; a

man at the height of his powers. A small shiver raked her skin, like the sensual rasp of a lover's tongue against sensitised flesh. Inside her head an image immediately formed: Sander's dark tanned hand cupping her own naked breast, his tongue curling round her swollen nipple. The small shiver became a racking shudder. Quickly Ruby tried to banish the image, closing down the computer screen. She was feeling nauseous again. Shakily, she made her way to the bathroom.

CHAPTER SIX

'I NOW pronounce you man and wife.'

It was over, done. There was no going back. Ruby was shaking inwardly, but she refused to let Sander see how upset she was.

Upset? A small tremor made her body shudder inside the cream Vera Wang dress she had not wanted to wear but which the personal shopper had included amongst her purchases and which for some reason she had felt obliged to wear. It was, after all, her wedding day. A fresh tremor broke through her self-control. What was the matter with her? What had she expected? Hearts and flowers? A declaration of undying devotion? This was Sander she was marrying, Sander who had not looked at her once during the brief ceremony in the anonymous register office, who couldn't have made it plainer how little he wanted her as his wife. Well, no more than she wanted him as her husband.

Sander looked down at Ruby's left hand. The ring he had just slipped onto her marriage finger was slightly loose, despite the fact that it should have fitted. She was far too thin and seemed to be getting thinner. But why should her fragility concern him?

It didn't. Women were adept at creating fictional images in order to deceive others. To her sons Ruby was no doubt a much loved mother, a constant and secure presence in their lives. At their age that had been his own feeling about his mother. Bitterness curled through him, spreading its poisonous infection.

In the years since the deaths of his parents he had often wondered if his father had given in so readily to his mother's financial demands because secretly he had loved her, even though he'd known she'd only despised him, and she, knowing that, had used his love against him. It was a fate he had sworn would never be his own.

And yet here he was married, and to a woman he already knew he could not trust—a woman who had given herself to him with such sensuality and intimacy that even now after so many years he was unable to strip from his memory the images she had left upon it. He had been a fool to let her get close enough to him once to do that. He wasn't going to let it happen again.

Neither of them spoke in the taxi taking them back to the hotel. Ruby already knew Sander had some business matters to attend to, which thankfully meant that she would have some time to herself in which to come to terms with the commitment she had just made.

After Sander had escorted them to the suite and then left without a word to her, after kissing the boys, Ruby reminded herself that she had not only walked willingly into this marriage, she was the one who had first suggested it.

The boys were tired—worn out, Ruby suspected, by the excitement of being in London. A short sleep would do them all good, and might help to ease her cramped, nauseous stomach and aching head.

After removing her wedding dress and pulling on her old dressing gown, she put the twins to bed. Once she had assured herself that they were asleep she went into her own bathroom, fumbling in her handbag for some headache tablets and accidentally removing the strip of birth control pills instead. They reminded her that although Sander might have made her take them she must not let him make her want him. Her hands shook as she replaced them to remove the pack of painkillers. Just that simple action had started her head pounding again, but thankfully this time at least she wasn't sick.

She was so tired that after a bath to help her relax she could barely dry herself, never mind bother to put on a nightdress. Instead she simply crawled beneath the duvet on her bed, falling asleep almost immediately.

Ruby woke up reluctantly, dragged from her sleep by a sense of nagging urgency. It only took her a matter of seconds to realise what had caused it. The silence. She couldn't hear the twins. How long had she been asleep? Her heart jolted anxiously into her ribs when she looked at her watch and realised that it was over three hours since she had tucked the twins into their beds. Why were they so quiet?

Trembling with apprehension, she pushed back the bedclothes, grabbing the towel she had discarded earlier and wrapping it around herself as she ran barefoot from her own room to the twins'.

It was empty. Her heart lurched sickeningly, and then started to beat frantically fast with fear.

On shaking legs Ruby ran through the suite, opening doors, calling their names, even checking the security lock on the main door to the suite just in case they had somehow opened it. All the time the hideous reality of what might have happened was lying in wait for her inside her head.

In the dreadful silence of the suite—only a parent could know and understand how a silence that should have been filled with the sound of children's voices could feel—she sank down onto one of the sofas.

The reason the twins weren't here must be because Sander had taken them. There could be no other explanation. He must have come back whilst she was asleep and seized his opportunity. He hadn't wanted to marry her any more than she had wanted to marry him. What he had wanted was the twins. His sons. And now he had them.

Were they already on a plane to the island? *His* island, where he made the laws and where she would never be able to reach them. He had their passports after all. A legal necessity, he had said, and she had stupidly accepted that.

Shock, grief, fear and anger—she could feel them all, but over and above those feelings was concern for her sons and fury that Sander could have done something so potentially harmful to them.

She could hear a noise: the sound of the main door to the suite opening, followed by the excited babble of two familiar voices.

The twins!

She was on her feet, hardly daring to believe that she wasn't simply imagining hearing them out of her own need, and then they were there, in the room with her, running towards her and telling her excitedly, 'Daddy took us to a café for our tea, because you were asleep,' bringing the smell of cold air in with them.

Dropping onto her knees, Ruby hugged them to her not trusting herself to speak, holding the small wriggling bodies tightly. They were her life, her heart, her everything. She could hardly bear to let them go.

Sander was standing watching her, making

her acutely conscious as she struggled to stand up that all that covered her nudity was the towel she had wrapped round her.

Going back to her bedroom, she discarded the towel and grabbed a clean pair of knickers before reaching for her old and worn velour dressing gown. She was too worked up and too anxious to get back to the twins as quickly as she could to care what she looked like or what Sander thought. The fact that he hadn't taken them as she had initially feared paled into insignificance compared with her realisation that he could have done so. Now that she had had a taste of what it felt like to think she had lost them, she knew more than ever that there was nothing she would not do or sacrifice to keep them with her.

Her hands trembled violently as she tied the belt on her dressing gown. From the sitting room she could hear the sound of cartoon voices from the television, and when she went back in the boys were sitting together, watching a children's TV programme, whilst Sander was seated at the small desk with his laptop open in front of him.

Neither of them had spoken, but the tension and hostility crackling in the air between them spoke a language they could both hear and understand.

Her headache might have gone, but it had been replaced with an equally sickening sense of guilt, Ruby acknowledged, when she sat down an hour later to read to the boys, now bathed and in bed. She watched them as they fell asleep after their bedtime story. Today something had happened that she had never experienced before. She had slept so deeply that she had not heard anything when Sander returned and took her sons. How could that be? How could she have been so careless of their safety?

She didn't want to leave them. She wanted to stay here all night with them.

The bedroom door opened. Immediately Ruby stiffened, whispering, 'What do you want?'

'I've come to say goodnight to my sons.'

'They're asleep.' She got up and walked to the door, intending to go through it and then close it, excluding him, but Sander was holding it and she was the one forced to leave and then watch as he went to kiss their sleeping faces.

Turning on her heel, Ruby headed for her own room. But before she stepped inside it her self-control broke and she whirled round, telling Sander, 'You had no right to take the boys out without asking me first.'

'They are my sons. I have every right. And as for telling you—'

Telling her, not asking her. Ruby noted his correction, consumed now by the kind of anger that followed the trauma of terrible shock and fear, which was a form of relief at discovering that the unthinkable hadn't happened after all.

'You were asleep.'

'You could have woken me. You *should* have woken me. It's my right as their mother to know where they are.'

'Your *right*? What about *their* rights? What about their right to have a mother who doesn't put her own needs first? I suppose a woman who goes out at night picking up men needs to sleep during the day. And knowing you as I do, I imagine that is what *you* do.'

Sickened by what he was implying, Ruby said fiercely, '*Knowing* me? You don't know me at all. And the unpleasant little scenario you have just outlined has never and would never take place. I have never so much as gone out at night and left the twins, never mind gone out picking up men. The reason I was asleep was because I haven't been feeling well—not that I expect you to believe me. You'd much rather make up something you can insult me with than listen to the truth.'

'I've had firsthand experience of the truth of what you are.'

Ruby's face burned. 'You're basing your judgement of me on one brief meeting, when I was—'

'Too drunk to know what you were doing?'

His cynical contempt was too much for Ruby's composure. For years she had tortured and tormented herself because of what she had done. She didn't need Sander weighing in to add to that self-punishment and pain. She shook her head in angry denial.

'Foolish and naive enough to want to create a fairy story out of something and someone belonging in reality to a horror story,' she said bitterly. Too carried away by the anger bursting past her self-control, she continued, 'You need not have wasted your contempt on me, because it can't possibly match the contempt I feel for myself, for deluding myself that you were someone special.'

Ruby felt sick and dizzy. Memories of what they had once shared were rushing in, roaring over her mental barriers and springing into vivid life inside her. She had been such a fool, so willing and eager to go to him, seeking in his arms the security and safety she had lost and thinking in her naivety that she would find them by binding herself to him in the most intimate way there was.

'So much drama,' Sander taunted her, 'and all of it so unnecessary, since I know it for the deceit that it is.'

'You are the one who is deceiving yourself by believing what you do,' Ruby threw at him emotionally.

'You dare to accuse *me* of self-deception?' Sander demanded, stepping towards her as he spoke, forcing her to step back into her bedroom. She backed up so quickly that she ended up standing on the trailing belt of her dressing gown. The soft, worn fabric gave way immediately, exposing the pale curve of her breast and the darker flesh of her nipple.

Sander saw what had happened before Ruby was aware of it herself, and his voice dropped to a cynical softness as he said, 'So that's what you want, is it? Same old Ruby. Well, why not? You certainly owe me something.'

Ruby's despairing, 'No!' was lost, crushed beneath the cruel strength of his mouth as it fastened on hers, and the sound of the door slamming as he pushed it closed was a death knell on her chances of escape.

Her robe quickly gave way to the swift expertise of Sander's determined hands, sliding from Ruby's body whilst he punished her with his kiss. In the mirror Sander could see the narrow curve of her naked back. Her skin, palely luminous, reminded him of the inside of the shells washed up on the beach below his home. Against his will old memories stirred, of how beneath his touch and against it she had trembled and then shuddered, calling out to him in open pleasure, so easily aroused by even the lightest caress. A wanton who had made no attempt to conceal the passion that drove her, or her own pleasure in his satisfaction of it, crying out to him to please her.

Sander drove his tongue between her lips as fiercely as he wanted to drive out her memory.

The honeyed sensuality of her mouth closed round him, inviting his tongue-tip's exploration of its sweetest hidden places. The simple plain white knickers she was wearing jarred against the raw sexuality of his own arousal. He wanted her naked and eager, stripped of the lies and deceit with which she was so keen to veil her own reality. He would make her admit to what she was, show her that he knew the true naked reality of her. His hands gripped her and held her, moving down over her body to push aside her protective covering.

Her figure was as perfect as it was possible for a woman's figure to be—or it would be if she carried a few more pounds, Sander acknowledged. From her shoulders, her torso narrowed down into a handspan waist before curving out into feminine hips and the high, rounded cheeks of her bottom. Her legs were long and slender, designed to wrap erotically and greedily around the man she chose to give her the pleasure she craved. Her breasts were full and soft, and he could remember how sensitive her nipples had been, the suckle of his mouth against them making her cry out in ecstasy.

Why was he tormenting himself with mere memories when she was here and his for the taking, her body already shivering in his hold with anticipation of the pleasure to come?

She was naked and in Sander's power. She should fight him and reject him, Ruby knew. She wanted to, but her body wanted something else. Her body wanted Sander.

Like some dark power conjured up by a master sorcerer desire swept through her, overwhelming reason and pride, igniting a need so intense that she felt as though an alien force were possessing her, dictating actions and reactions it was impossible for her to control.

It was as though in Sander's arms she became a different person—a wildly passionate, elementally sensual woman of such intensity that everything she was crystallised in the act of being taken by him and taking him in turn.

It might be her wish to fight what possessed her, but it was also her destiny to submit to it as Sander's mouth moved from its fierce possession of hers to an equally erotic exploration of her throat, lingering on the pulse there that so recklessly gave away her arousal.

It was not enough to have her naked to his gaze and his touch. He needed to have the feel of her against his own skin. She was an ache, a need, a compulsion that wouldn't allow him to rest until he had conquered her and she had submitted to his mastery of her pleasure. He wanted, needed, to hear her cry out that desire to him before he could allow himself to submit to his own desire for her. He needed her to offer up her pleasure to him before he could lose himself within her and take his own.

He was caught in a trap as old as Eve herself—caught and held in the silken web of a desire only she had the power to spin. The savagery of his anger that this should be so was only matched by the savagery of his need for the explosion of fevered sensuality now possessing them both. It was a form of madness, a fever, a possession he couldn't escape.

Scooping her up in his arms, Sander carried Ruby to the bed, watching her watch him as he placed her on it and then wrenched off his own clothes, seeing the way her eyes betrayed her reaction to the sight of him, naked and ready for her.

Her eyes dark and wide with delight, Ruby reached out to touch the formidable thickness of Sander's erection, marvelling at the texture of his flesh beneath her fingers. Engrossed and entranced, she stroked her fingertips over the length of him, easing back the hooded cover to reveal the sensitive flesh beneath it, not the woman she knew as herself any more, but instead a Ruby who was possessed by the powerful dark force of their shared desire—a Ruby whose breath quickened and whose belly tightened in pleasurable longing.

She looked up at Sander and saw in his eyes the same need she knew was in her own. She lifted her hand from his body, and as though it had been a signal to him he pushed her back on the bed, following her down, shaping and moulding her breasts with his hands, feeding her need for the erotic pleasure she knew he could give her with the heat of his lips and his tongue on her nipples, until she arched up against him, whimpering beneath the unbearable intensity of her own pleasure.

The feel of his hand cupping her sex wasn't just something she welcomed. It was something she needed.

Her body was wet and ready for him, just as it had been before. Just for a heartbeat the mistrust that was his mother's legacy to him surfaced past Sander's desire. There must not be another unwanted conception.

'The pill—' he began,

Ruby nodded her head.

A sheen of perspiration gleamed on his tanned flesh, and the scent of his arousal was heightening her own. It was frightening, this intensity of desire, this sharpening and focusing of her senses so that only Sander filled them. It had frightened her six years ago and it still frightened her now. The need he aroused within her demanded that she gave everything of herself over to him—all that she was, every last bit of her. The verbal demand he was making now was nothing compared with that.

'Yes. I'm taking it.'

'You swear?'

'I swear…'

Sander heard the unsteady note of need trembling in her voice. She was impatient for him, but no more than he was for her. He had fought to hold back the tide of longing for her from the minute he had seen her again. It had mocked his efforts to deny it, and now it was overwhelming him, the fire burning within him consuming him. Right now, in this heartbeat of time, nothing else mattered. He was in the grip of a force so powerful that he had to submit to it.

They moved together, without the need for

words, movement matching movement, a duel of shared anger and longing. Her body welcomed his, holding it, sheathing it, moving with it and against it, demanding that he move faster and deeper, driving them both to that place from which they could soar to the heavens and then fall back to earth.

It was here now—that shuddering climax of sensation, gripping her, gripping Sander, causing the spurting spill of the seeds of new life within her. Only this time there would be no new life because she was on the pill.

They lay together in the darkness, their breathing unsteady and audible in the silence.

Now—now when it was over, and his flesh was washed with the cold reality of how quickly he had given in to his need for her— Sander was forced to accept the truth. He could not control the physical desire she aroused in him. It had overwhelmed him, and it would overwhelm him again. That knowledge was a bitter blow to his pride.

Without looking at her, he told her emotionlessly, 'From now on I am the only man you will have sex with. Is that understood? I will not have my wife shaming me by offering herself to other men. And to ensure that you don't I shall make it my business to see to it that your eager appetite for sexual pleasure is kept satisfied.'

Sander knew that his words were merely a mask for the reality that he could neither bear the thought of her with another man nor control his own desire for her, no matter how much he despised himself for his weakness.

Ruby could feel her face burning with humiliation. She wanted to tell him that she didn't understand what happened to her when she was in his arms. She wanted to tell him that other men did not have the same effect on her. She wanted to tell him that he was the only man she had ever had sex with. But she knew that he wouldn't listen.

Later, alone in his own room, Sander tried to explain to himself why the minute he touched

Ruby he became filled with a compulsion to possess her. His desire for her was stronger than his resolve to resist it, and he couldn't. What she made him feel and want was unique to her, loath as he was to admit that.

CHAPTER SEVEN

GIVEN Sander's wealth, Ruby had half expected
that they might fly first-class to the island—but
what she had not expected was that they would
be travelling in the unimagined luxury of a
private jet, with them the only passengers on
board. But that was exactly what had happened,
and now, with the boys taken by the steward to
sit with the captain for a few minutes, she and
Sander were alone in the cabin, with its cream
leather upholstery and off-white carpets.

'The money it must cost to own and run something like this would feed hundreds of poor
families,' Ruby couldn't stop herself from saying.

Her comment, and the unspoken accusation
it held, made Sander frown. He had never once

heard his mother express concern for 'poor families', and the fact that Ruby had done so felt like a sharp paper cut on the tender skin of his judgement of her—something small and insignificant in one sense, but in another something he could not ignore, no matter how much he might want to do so.

To his own disbelief he found himself defending his position, telling her, 'I don't actually own it. I merely belong to a small consortium of businessmen who share and charter it when they need it. As for feeding the poor—on the island we operate a system which ensures that no one goes hungry and that every child has access to an education matched to their skills and abilities. We also have a free health service and a good pension system—the latter two schemes put in place by my father.'

Why on earth did he think he had to justify anything he did to *Ruby*?

* * *

It was dark when their flight finally put down on the island, the darkness obscuring their surroundings apart from what they could see in the blaze of the runway lights as they stepped down from the plane and into the warm velvet embrace of the Mediterranean evening. A soft breeze ruffled the boys' hair as they clung to Ruby's sides, suddenly uncertain and unsure of themselves. A golf cart type of vehicle was their transport for the short distance to the arrivals building, where Sander shook hands with the officials waiting to greet him before ushering them outside again to the limousine waiting for them. It was Sander who lifted the sleepy children into it, settling Harry on his lap and then putting his free arm around Freddie, whilst Ruby was left to sit on her own. Her arms felt empty without the twins, and she felt a maternal urge to reach for them, but she resisted it, not wanting to disturb them now that they were asleep.

The headache and subsequent nausea it had

caused her had thankfully not returned, although she still didn't feel one hundred percent.

The car moved swiftly down a straight smooth road before eventually turning off it onto a more winding road, on one side of which Ruby could see the sea glinting in the moonlight. On the other side of them was a steep wall of rock, which eventually gave way to an old fashioned fortress-like city wall, with a gateway in it through which they drove, past tall buildings and then along a narrow street which broadened out into the large formal square Ruby had seen on the internet.

'This is the main square of the city, with the Royal Palace up ahead of us,' Sander informed her.

'Is that where we'll be living?' Ruby asked apprehensively.

Sander shook his head.

'No. The palace is used only for formal occasions now, and as an administrative centre. After my grandfather died I had my own villa built just outside the city. I don't care for pomp and circumstance. My people's quality of life is what is important to me, just as it was to my father. I cannot expect to have their respect if I do not give them mine.'

Ruby looked away from him. His comments showed the kind of attitude she admired, but how could she allow herself to admire Sander? It was bad enough that he could arouse her physically without her being vulnerable to him emotionally as well.

'The city must be very old,' she said instead.

'Very,' Sander agreed.

As always when he returned to the island after an absence, he was torn in opposing directions. He loved the island and its people, but he also had the painful memories of his childhood here to contend with.

In an effort to banish them and concentrate on something else, he told Ruby, 'The Phoenicians and the Egyptians traded here, just as they did with our nearest neighbour Cyprus. Like Cyprus, we too have large deposits of copper here, and possession of the island was fought over fiercely during the Persian wars. In the end a marriage alliance between the opposing forces brought the fighting to an end. That has traditionally been the way in which territorial disputes have been settled here—' He broke off to look at her as he heard the small sound Ruby made.

Ruby shivered, unable to stop herself from saying, 'It must have been dreadful for the poor brides who were forced into marriage.'

'It is not the exclusive right of *your* sex to detest a forced marriage.'

Sander's voice was so harsh that the twins stirred against him in their sleep, focusing Ruby's attention on her sons, although she was still able to insist defensively, 'Historically a man has always had more rights within marriage than a woman.'

'The right to freedom of choice is enshrined in the human psyche of both sexes and should be respected above all other things,' Sander insisted.

Ruby looked at him in disbelief. 'How can you say that after the way you have forced me…?'

'You were the one who insisted on marriage.'

'Because I had no other choice.'

'There is always a choice.'

'Not for a mother. She will always put her children first.'

Her voice held a conviction that Sander told himself had to be false, and the cynical look he gave her said as much, causing Ruby's face to burn as she remembered how she had fallen asleep, leaving the twins unprotected.

Looking away from her, Sander thought angrily that Ruby might *think* she had deceived him by claiming her reason for insisting he married her was that she wanted to protect her sons, but he knew perfectly well that it was the fact that she believed marriage to him would give her a share in his wealth. That was what she really wanted to protect.

But she had signed a prenuptial agreement that barred her from making any claim on his money should they ever divorce, an inner voice defended her unexpectedly. She probably thought she could have the prenup set aside, Sander argued against it. Her children loved her, the inner voice pointed out. They would not exhibit the love and trust they did if she was a bad mother. He had loved *his* mother at their age, Sander pointed out. But he had hardly seen his mother or spent much time with her. She had been an exotic stranger, someone he had longed to see, and yet when he had seen her she had made him feel anxious to please her, and wary of her sudden petulant outbursts if he accidentally touched her expensive clothes. Anna, who was now in charge of the villa's household, had been more of a true mother—not just to him, but to all of them.

As Anna had been with them, Ruby was with the twins all the time. Logically he had to admit that it simply wasn't possible for anyone to carry out the pretence of being a caring parent twenty-four seven if it was just an act. A woman who loved both money and her children? Was that possible? It galled Sander that he should even be asking himself that question. What was the matter with him? He knew exactly what she was—why should he now be finding reasons to think better of her?

Sander looked away from Ruby and out into the darkness beyond the car window. The boys were soft warm weights against his body. His sons, and he loved them utterly and completely, no matter who or what their mother was. It was for their sakes that he wanted to find some good in her, for their sakes that his inner voice was trying to insist she was a good mother—for what caring father would *not* want that for his children, especially when that father knew what it was to have a mother who did not care.

Was it her imagination, or were the twins already turning more to Sander than they did to her? Miserably Ruby stared through the car window next to her. Whilst they had been talking they had left the city behind and were now travelling along another coastal road, with the sea to one side of them. But where previously there had been steep cliffs now the land rolled more gently away from the road.

It was far too late and far too selfish of her to wish that Sander had not come back into her life, Ruby admitted as the silence between them grew, filled by Sander's contempt for her and entrapping her in her own ever-present guilt. It was that guilt for having conceived the twins so carelessly and thoughtlessly that had in part brought her here, Ruby recognised. Guilt and her overwhelming desire to give her sons the same kind of happy, unshadowed, secure childhood in a family protected by two loving parents that she herself had enjoyed until her parents' death. But that security had been ripped from her. Her heart started to thud in a mixture of remembered pain and fierce hope that her sons would never experience what she had.

On his side of the luxurious leather upholstered car Sander stared out into the darkness—

a darkness that for him was populated by the ghosts of his own past. In his grandfather's day the family had lived in the palace, unable to speak to either their parents or their grandfather unless those adults chose to seek them out. Yet despite maintaining his own distance from Sander and his siblings, their grandfather had somehow managed to know every detail of his grandchildren's lives, regularly sending for them so that he could list their flaws and faults and petty childhood crimes.

His sister and brother had been afraid of their grandfather, but Sander, the eldest child and ultimately the heir to his grandfather's shipping empire, had quickly learned that the best way to deal with his grandparent was to stand up to him. Sander's pride had been honed on the whetstone of his grandfather's mockery and baiting, as he'd constantly challenged Sander to prove himself to him whilst at the same time having no compunction about seeking to destroy his pride in himself to maintain his own superiority.

An English boarding school followed by university had given him a welcome respite from his grandfather's overbearing and bullying ways, but it had been after Sander had left university and started work in the family business that the real clashes between them had begun.

The continuation of the family and the business had been all that really mattered to his grandfather. His son and his grandchildren had been merely pawns to be used to further that cause. Sander had grown up hearing his grandfather discussing the various merits of young heiresses whom Sander might be wise to marry, but what he had learned from his mother, allied to his own naturally alpha personality and the time he had spent away from the island whilst he was at school and university, had made Sander determined not to allow his grandfather to bully him into marriage as he had done his father.

There had been many arguments between them on the subject, with his grandfather constantly trying to manipulate and bully Sander into meeting one or other of the young women he'd deemed suitable to be the mother of the next heir. In the end, infuriated and sickened by his grandfather's attempts at manipulation and coercion, Sander had announced to his grandfather that he was wasting his time as he never intended to marry, since he already had an heir in his brother.

His grandfather had then threatened to disinherit him, and Sander had challenged him to go ahead, telling him that he would find employment with one of their rivals. There the matter had rested for several weeks, giving Sander the impression that finally his grandfather had realised that he was not going to be controlled as his own parents had been controlled. But then, virtually on the eve of a long planned visit by Sander to the UK, to meet with some important clients in Manchester, he had discovered that his grandfather was planning to use his absence to advise the press of an impending engagement between Sander and the young widow of another ship-owner. Apart from anything else Sander knew that the young widow in question had a string of lovers and a serious drug habit, but neither of those potential drawbacks had been of any interest to his grandfather.

Of course Sander had confronted his grandfather, and both of them had been equally angry with the other. His grandfather had refused to back down, and Sander had warned him that if he went ahead with a public announcement then he would refute that announcement equally publicly.

By the time he had reached Manchester Sander's anger hadn't cooled and his resolve to live his own life had actively hardened—to the extent that he had decided that on his return to Greece he was going to cut all ties with his grandfather and set up his own rival business from scratch.

And it had been in that frame of mind, filled

with a dangerous mix of emotions, that he had met Ruby. He could see her now, eyeing him up from the other side of the crowded club, her blonde hair as carefully tousled as her lip-glossed mouth had been deliberately pouted. The short skirt she'd worn had revealed slender legs, her tight top had been pulled in to display her tiny waist, and the soft rounded upper curves of her breasts had been openly on display. In short she had looked no different from the dozens of other eager, willing and easily available young women who came to the club specifically because it was known to be a haunt for louche young footballers and their entourages.

The only reason Sander had been in the club had been to meet a contact who knew people Sander thought might be prepared to give his proposed new venture some business. Whilst he was there Sander had received a phone call from a friend, urging him not to act against his own best interests. Immediately Sander had known that somehow his grandfather had got wind of what he was planning, and that someone had betrayed him. Fury—against his grandfather, against all those people in his life he had trusted but who had betrayed him—had overwhelmed him, exploding through his veins, pulsing against all constraints like the molten heat of a volcano building up inside him until it could not be contained any longer, the force of it erupting to spew its dangerous contents over everything in its path. And Ruby had been in the path of that fury, a readymade sacrifice to his anger, all too willing to allow him to use her for whatever purpose he chose.

All it had taken to bring her to his side had been one cynical and deliberately lingering glance. She had leaned close to him in the crush of the club, her breath smelling of vodka and her skin of soap. He remembered how that realisation had momentarily checked him. The other girls around her had reeked of cheap scent. He had offered to buy her a drink and she had shaken her head, looking at him with such openly hungry eyes that her lack of self-respect had further inflamed his fury. He had questioned to himself why girls like her preferred to use their bodies to support themselves instead of their brains, giving themselves to men not directly for money but in the hope that they would end up as the girlfriend of a wealthy man.

Well, there had been no place in his life for a 'girlfriend', but right then there *had* been a rage, a tension inside him that he knew the use of her body in the most basic way there was would do much to alleviate. He had reached for his drink—not his first of the evening— finished it with one swallow, before turning to her and saying brusquely, 'Come on.'

A bump in the road woke the twins up, and Harry's 'Are we there yet?' dragged Sander's thoughts from the past to the present.

'Nearly,' he answered him. 'We're turning into the drive to the villa now.'

As he spoke the car swung off the road at

such a sharp angle that Ruby slid along the leather seat, almost bumping her head on the side of the car. Unlike her, though, the twins were safe, protected by the arms Sander had tightened around them the minute the car had started to turn. Sander loved the twins, but he did not love her.

The pain that gripped her caught Ruby off guard. She wasn't jealous of her own sons, was she? Of course not. The last thing she wanted was Sander's arms around *her*, she told herself angrily as they drove through a pair of ornate wrought-iron gates and then down a long straight drive bordered with Cypress trees and illuminated by lights set into the ground.

At the end of the drive was a gravelled rectangle, and beyond that the villa itself, discreetly floodlit to reveal its elegant modern lines and proportions.

'Anna, who is in charge of the household, will have everything ready for you and the twins. She and Georgiou, her husband, who has driven us here, look after the villa and its gardens between them. They have their own private quarters over the garage block, which is separate from the villa itself,' Sander informed Ruby as the car crunched to a halt over the gravel.

Almost immediately the front door to the villa was opened to reveal a tall, well-built woman with dark hair streaked with grey and a serene expression.

It gave Ruby a fierce pang of emotion to see the way the twins automatically put their hands in Sander's and not her own as they walked with their father towards her. Her smile of welcome for Sander was one of love and delight, and Ruby watched in amazement as Sander returned her warm hug with obvious affection. Somehow it was not what she had expected. Anna—Ruby assumed the woman was Anna—was plainly far more to Sander than merely the person who was in charge of his household.

Now she was bending down to greet the boys, not overwhelming them by hugging them as she had Sander, Ruby noted approvingly, but instead waiting for them to go to her.

Sander gave them a little push and told them, 'This is Anna. She looked after me when I was a boy, and now she will look after you.'

Immediately Ruby's maternal hackles rose. Her sons did not need Anna or anyone else to look after them. They had her. She stepped forward herself, placing one hand on each of her son's shoulders, and then was completely disarmed when Anna smiled warmly and approvingly at her, as though welcoming what she had done rather than seeing it as either a challenge or a warning.

When Sander introduced her to Anna as his wife, it was obvious that Anna had been expecting them. What had Sander said to his family and those who knew him about the twins? How had he explained away the fact that he was suddenly producing them—and her? Ruby didn't know but she did know that Anna at least was delighted to welcome the twins as Sander's sons. It was plain she was ready to adore and spoil them, and was going to end up completely under their thumbs.

'Anna will show you round the villa and provide you and the boys with something to eat,' Sander informed Ruby.

He said something in Greek to Anna, who beamed at him and nodded her head vigorously, and then he was gone, striding across the white limestone floor of the entrance hall and disappearing through one of the dark wooden doors set into the white walls.

That feeling gripping her wasn't a sense of loss, was it? A feeling of being abandoned? A longing for Sander to return, because without him their small family was incomplete? Because without him *she* was incomplete?

As soon as the treacherous words whispered across her mind Ruby stiffened in denial of them. But they had left an echo that wasn't easily silenced, reminding her of all that she had suffered when she had first been foolish enough to think that he cared about her.

CHAPTER EIGHT

'I'll show you your rooms first,' Anna told Ruby, 'and then perhaps you would like a cup of tea before you see the rest of the villa?'

There was something genuinely warm and kind and, well, *motherly* about Anna that had Ruby's initial wary hostility melting away as they walked together up the marble stairs, the twins in between them.

When they reached the top and saw the long wide landing stretching out ahead of them the twins looked at Ruby hopefully.

Shaking her head, she began, 'No—no running inside—' Only to have Anna smile broadly at her.

'This is their home now, they may run if you permit it,' she told her.

'Very well,' Ruby told them, relieved by Anna's understanding of the need of two young children to let off steam, and both women watched as the boys ran down the corridor.

'Looking at them is like looking at Sander when he was a similar age, except that—' Anna stopped, her smile fading.

'Except that what?' Ruby asked her, sensitively defensive of any possible criticism being lodged against her precious sons.

As though she had guessed what Ruby was thinking, Anna patted Ruby on the arm.

'You are a good mother—anyone can see that. Your goodness and your love for them is reflected in your sons' smiles. Sander's mother was not like that. Her children were a duty she resented, and they all, especially Sander, learned young not to turn to their mother for love and comfort.'

Anna's quiet words formed an image inside Ruby's head she didn't want to see—an image of a young and vulnerable Sander, a child with sadness in his eyes, standing alone and hurt by his mother's lack of love for him.

The boys raced back to them, putting an end to any more confidences from Anna about Sander's childhood, and Ruby's sympathy for the child that Sander had been was swiftly pushed to one side when she discovered that the two of them were going to be sharing a bedroom and a bed.

Why did she feel so unnerved and apprehensive? Ruby asked herself later, after Anna had helped her put the twins to bed and she was in the kitchen, drinking the fresh cup of tea Anna had insisted on making for her. Sander had already made it plain that she must accept that their marriage would include sexual intimacy. They both already knew that she wanted him, and she had already suffered the humiliation *that* had brought her, so what was there left for her to fear?

There was emotional vulnerability, Ruby admitted. With her sexual vulnerability to Sander there was already a danger that she could become sexually dependent on him, and that was bad enough. If she also became emotionally vulnerable to him might she not then become emotionally dependent on him? Where had that thought come from? She was a million miles from feeling anything emotional for Sander, wasn't she?

Excusing herself to Anna, Ruby explained that she wanted to go up and check the twins were still sleeping as they had left them, not wanting them to wake alone in such new surroundings.

The twins' bedroom, like the one she was to share with Sander, looked out onto a courtyard and an infinity pool with the sea beyond it. But whilst Sander's bedroom had glass doors that opened out onto the patio area that surrounded the pool, the boys' room merely had a window—a safety feature for which she was extremely grateful. Glass bedroom doors, a swimming pool, and two adventurous five-year-olds were a mix that would arouse anxiety in any protective mother.

She needn't have worried about the twins. They were both sleeping soundly, their faces turned toward one another. Love for them filled her. But as she bent towards them to kiss them it wasn't their faces she could see but that of another young child, a child whose dark eyes, so like those of her sons, were shadowed with pain and angry pride. Sander's eyes. They still held that angry pride now, as an adult, when he looked at her. And the pain? Her question furrowed Ruby's brow. Emotional pain was not something she had previously equated with Sander. But the circumstances a child experienced growing up affected it all its life. She believed that wholeheartedly. If she hadn't done so then she would not feel as strongly as she did about Sander being a part of the twins' lives. So what had happened to Sander's pain? Was it buried somewhere deep inside him? A sad, sore place that could never heal? A wound that was the cruellest wound of all to a child—the lack of its mother's love?

Confused by her own thoughts, Ruby left her sleeping sons. She was tired and ready for bed herself. Her heart started beating unsteadily. Tired and ready for bed? Ready to share Sander's bed?

The villa was beautifully decorated. The guest suite Anna had shown Ruby, and in which she would have preferred to be sleeping, was elegantly modern, the clean lines of its furniture softened by gauzy drapes, the cool white and taupe of the colour scheme broken up with touches of Mediterranean blues and greens in the artwork adorning the walls.

From the twins' room Ruby made her way to the room she was sharing with Sander—not because she wanted to look again at the large bed and let her imagination taunt her with images of what they would share there, but because she needed to unpack, Ruby told herself firmly. Only when she opened the door to the bedroom the cases that had been there before had vanished, and from the *en suite* bathroom through the open door she could smell the sharp citrus scent of male soap and hear the sound of the shower.

Had Sander had her cases removed? Had he told Anna that he didn't want to share a room with her? Relief warred with a jolt of female protectiveness of her position as his wife. She liked Anna, but she didn't want the other woman to think that Sander was rejecting her. That would be humiliating. More humiliating than being forced in the silence of the night to cry out in longing to a husband who could arouse in her a hunger she could not control?

Ruby moved restlessly from one foot to the other, and then froze as the door to the *en suite* bathroom opened fully and Sander walked into the bedroom.

He had wrapped a towel round his hips. His body was still damp from his shower, and the white towel threw into relief the powerful tanned male V shape of his torso and the breadth of his shoulders, tapering down over

strong muscles to his chest, to the hard flatness
of his belly. The shadowing of dark hair slicked
wetly against his skin emphasised a maleness
that had Ruby trapped in its sensual spell. She
wanted to look away from him. She wanted not
to remember, not to feel, not to be so easily and
completely overwhelmed by the need that just
looking at him brought back to simmering heat.
But she didn't have that kind of self-control.
Instead of satiating her desire for him, what
they had already shared seemed only to have increased her need for him.

Her own intense sensuality bewildered her.
She had lived for six years without ever once
wanting to have sex, and yet now she only had
to look at Sander to be consumed by this alien
desire that seemed to have taken possession of
her. Possession. Just thinking the word increased the heat licking at her body, tightening
the pulse flickering eagerly deep inside her.

It was Ruby's fault that he wanted her, Sander
told himself. It was she, with her soft mouth

and her hungry gaze, with her eagerness, who was responsible for his own inability to control the savage surging of his need to possess her. It was because of her that he felt this ache, this driven, agonising urgency that unleashed within him something he barely recognised as part of himself.

Like a wild storm, a tornado threatening to suck them both up into its perilous grasp, Ruby could feel the pressure of their combined desire. Fear filled her. She didn't want this. It shamed and weakened her. Dragging her gaze from Sander's body, she started to run towards the door in blind panic. But Sander moved faster, reaching the door before her, and the impetus of her panic slammed her into his body, the impact shocking through her.

Tears of anger—against herself, against him, and against the aching desire flooding her—filled her eyes and she curled her hands into small fists and beat them impotently against his chest. Sander seized hold of her wrists.

'I don't want to feel like this,' she cried, agonized.

'But you do. You want this, and you want me,' he told her, before he took the denial from her lips with the ruthless pressure of his own.

Just the taste of her unleashed within him a hunger he couldn't control. The softness of her lips, the sound she made when he kissed her, the way her whole body shuddered against his with longing, drove him in what felt like a form of madness, a need, to a place where nothing else existed or mattered, where bringing her desire within the control of his ability to satisfy it felt as though it was what he had been born for.

Each sound she made, each shudder of pleasure her body gave, each urgent movement against his touch that begged silently for more became a goal he had to reach—a test of his maleness he had to master, so that he would always be the only man she desired, *his* pleasuring of her the only pleasure that could satisfy her. Something about the pale silkiness of her skin as he slid her clothes from it made him want to touch it over and over again. His hands already knew the shape and texture of her breasts, but that knowing only made him want to feel their soft weight even more. His lips and tongue and teeth might have aroused the swollen darkness of her nipples to previous pleasure, but now he wanted to recreate that pleasure. He wanted to slide his hand over the flatness of her belly and feel her suck it in as she fought to deny the effect of his touch and lost that fight. He wanted to part the slender thighs and feel them quiver, hear the small moan from between her lips, watch as she tried and failed to stop her thighs from opening eagerly to allow him the intimacy of her sex. He loved the way her soft, delicately shaped outer lips, so primly folded, opened to the slow stroke of his fingers, her wetness eagerly awaiting him.

A shocked cry of protest streaked with primitive longing burst from Ruby's throat as Sander gave in to the demand of his own arousal and moved down her body, to kiss the soft flesh on the inside of her thighs and then stroke the tip of his tongue the length of the female valley his skilled fingers had laid bare to his caress.

Waves of pleasure were racing through her, dragging her back to a level of sensuality where she was as out of her depth as a fledgling swimmer swept out by the tide into deep water. Each stroke of his tongue-tip against the most sensitive part of her took her deeper, until her own pleasure was swamping her, pulling her down into its embrace, until the rhythm it imposed on her was all that she knew, her response to it dictated and controlled by the lap of Sander's tongue as finally it overwhelmed her and she was drowning in it, giving herself over completely to it.

Later, filling her with his aching flesh, feeling her desire catch fire again as her body moved with his, inciting him towards his own destruction, Sander knew with razor-sharp clarity, in

the seconds before he cried out in the exulta-
tion of release, that what he was doing might
be trapping her in her desire for him but it was
also feeding his need for her.

CHAPTER NINE

FROM the shade of the vine-covered pergola, Ruby watched the twins as they splashed in the swimming pool under Sander's watchful eye. It was just over six weeks now since they had arrived on the island, and the twins were loving their new life. They worshipped Sander. He was a good father, Ruby was forced to admit, giving them his time and attention, and most important of all his love. She glanced towards the house. Anna would be bringing their lunch out to them soon. A prickle of despair trickled down her spine as chilling as cold water.

This morning she was finally forcing herself to confront the possibility that she might be pregnant! The breakfasts she had been unable to eat in the morning, the tiredness that engulfed her every afternoon, the slight swelling of her breasts—all could have other explanations, but her missed period was now adding to the body of evidence.

Could she really be pregnant? Her heart jumped sickeningly inside her chest. There must be no more children, Sander had said. She must take the contraceptive pill. She had done, without missing a single one, but her symptoms were exactly the same as those she had experienced with the twins. Sander would be angry—furious, even—but what could he do? She was his wife, they were married, and she was having his child. A child she already knew he would not want.

Ruby could feel anxiety-induced nausea clogging her throat and causing perspiration to break out on her forehead. Was she right in thinking that Anna already suspected? Anna was an angel, wonderful with the children—almost a grandmother to them. After all, she had mothered Sander and his sister and brother. Somehow she seemed to know when Ruby was feeling tired and not very well, taking charge of the twins for her, giving her a kind pat when she fell back on the fiction that her lack of energy and nausea were the result of their move to a hot climate.

Sander was getting the twins out of the pool. Anna had arrived with their lunch. Determinedly, Ruby pushed her anxiety to one side.

Sander was used to working at home when he needed to, but since he had brought Ruby and his sons to the island he had discovered that he actually preferred to work at home. So that he could be with his sons, or so that he could be with Ruby? That was nonsense. A stupid question which he could not bring himself to answer.

Angrily he tried to concentrate on the screen in front of him. This afternoon he was finding it hard to concentrate on the e-mails he should be answering. Because he was thinking about

Ruby? If he was then it was because of the conversation he had had with Anna earlier in the day, when she had commented on what a good mother Ruby was.

'A good mother and a good wife,' had been her exact words. 'You are a lucky man.'

Anna was a shrewd judge of character. She had never liked his mother, and she had protected them all from their grandfather's temper whenever she could. She had given him the only female love he had ever known. Homely, loyal Anna liked and approved of Ruby, a woman with more in common with his mother than she had with her.

Sander frowned. He might have seen the financially grasping side of Ruby that echoed the behaviour of his mother, but he had also seen her with the twins, and he was forced to admit that she *was* a loving and protective mother—a mother who gave her love willingly and generously to her sons…just as she gave herself willingly and generously to him…

Now what was he thinking? He was a fool if he started allowing himself to believe that. But did he want to believe it? No, Sander denied himself. Why should he want to believe that she gave him anything? Only a weak man or a fool allowed himself to think like that, and he was neither. But didn't the fact that he couldn't stop himself from wanting her reveal the worst kind of male weakness?

Wasn't the truth that even though he had tried to deny it to himself he had not been able to forget her? From that first meeting the memory of her had lain in his mind like a thorn in his flesh, driven in too deeply to be easily removed, the pain activated whenever an unwary movement caused it to make its presence felt.

He had taken her and used her as a release for his pent-up fury after his argument with his grandfather, telling himself that his behaviour was justified because she herself had sought him out.

Inside his head Sander could hear his grandfather's raised voice, see the fist he had
smashed down onto his desk in his rage that
Sander should defy him.

Sander moved restlessly in his computer
chair. It was too late now to regret allowing
himself to recall that final argument with his
grandfather and the events that had followed it.
Far too late. Because the past was here with
him, invading his present and filling it with
unwanted memories, and he was back in that
Manchester hotel room, watching Ruby sleep
curled up against him.

His mobile had started to ring in the grey light
of the dawn. She had protested in her sleep as he'd
moved away from her but she hadn't woken up.

The call had been from Anna, her anxiety and
shock reaching him across the miles as she told
him that she had found his grandfather collapsed on the floor of his office and that he was
on his way to hospital.

Sander had moved as quickly as he could,

waking Ruby and telling her brusquely that he wanted her out of his bed, his room and the hotel, using her yet again as a means of expelling the mingled guilt and anger the phone call had brought him.

She had looked shocked and uncomprehending, he remembered, no doubt having hoped for rather more from him than a few brief hours in bed. Then tears had welled up in her eyes and she had tried to cling to him. Irritated that she wasn't playing by the rules, he had thrust her off, reaching into his jacket pocket for his wallet and removing several crisp fifty-pound notes from it. It had increased his irritation when she had started to play the drama queen, backing off from him, shaking her head, looking at him as though he had stamped on a kitten, not offered her a very generous payment for her services.

His terse, 'Get dressed—unless you want the hotel staff to evict you as you are,' had had the desired effect. But even so he had escorted her downstairs and out to the taxi rank outside the hotel himself, putting her into a cab and then watching to make sure that she had actually left before completing his arrangements to get home.

As it turned out his grandfather had died within minutes of reaching the hospital, from a second major heart attack.

In his office Sander had found the document his grandfather had obviously been working on before he collapsed, and had seen that it was a notice to the papers stating that Sander was on the point of announcing his engagement. His guilt had evaporated. His guilt but not his anger. And yet despite everything Sander had still mourned him. Evidence of the same weakness that was undermining him now with regard to Ruby. A leopard did not change its spots just because someone was foolish enough to want it to do so.

After his grandfather's death Sandra had renewed his vow to himself to remain single.

How fate must have been laughing at him

then, knowing that the seeds of his own destiny had already been sown and had taken root.

He turned back to the computer, but it was no use. Once opened, the door to his memories of that fateful night with Ruby could not be closed.

The hotel bedroom, with its dark furniture, had been shadowed and silent, the heavy drapes deadening the sound of the traffic outside and yet somehow at the same time emphasising the unsteadiness of Ruby's breathing—small, shallow breaths that had lifted her breasts against her tight, low-cut top. The light from the standard lamp—switched on when the bed had been turned down for the night—had outlined the prominence of her nipples. When she had seen him looking at them she had lifted her hands towards her breasts, as though to protect them from his gaze. He could remember how that simple action had intensified his anger at her denial of everything she was about, in-furiating him in the same way that his grand-father had. The raging argument he'd had with his grandfather earlier that day had still been fresh in his mind. The two angers had met and joined together, doubling the intensity of his fury, driving him with a ferocious and over-powering need to possess her.

He had gone to her and pulled down her hands. Her body had trembled slightly in his hold. Had he hesitated then, trying to check the raging torrent within him, or did he just want to think that he had? The image he was creating of himself was that of a man out of control, unable to halt the force of his own emotions. In another man it would have filled him with distaste. But Ruby, he remembered, had stepped closer to him, not away from him, and it had been then that he had removed her top, taking with it her bra, leaving her breasts exposed. His actions had been instinctive, born of rage rather than desire, but somehow the sight of her nakedness, her breasts so perfectly shaped, had transmuted that rage into an equally intense surge of need—to touch them and caress them, to possess the flaunting sensuality of their tip tilted temptation.

They had both drawn in a breath, as though sharing the same thoughts and the same desire, and the tension of that desire had stretched their self-control until the air around them had almost thrummed with the vibration of it. Then Ruby had made a small sound in the back of her throat, and as though it had been some kind of signal to his senses his self-control had snapped. He had reached for her, no words needed as he'd kissed her, feeling her tremble in his arms as he probed the softly closed line of her lips. She had deliberately kept them closed in order to torment him. But two could play that game, and so, instead of forcing them to give way, he had tormented them into doing so, with soft, deliberately brief kisses, until Ruby had reached for the back of his neck, her fingers curling into his hair, and whimpered with protesting need against his mouth.

Sander closed his eyes and opened them

again as he recalled the surge of male triumph that had seized him then and the passion it had carried with it—a feeling he had never experienced either before Ruby or after her, surely originating from his anger against his grandfather and nothing else. Certainly not from some special effect that only Ruby could have on his senses. The very thought of that was enough to have him shifting angrily in his seat. No woman would *ever* be allowed to have that kind of power over him. Because he feared what might happen to him once he allowed himself to want a woman with that kind of intensity?

Better to return to his memories than to pursue *that* train of thought, Sander decided.

As they had kissed he had been able to feel Ruby's naked breasts pressed up against him. He had slipped his hands between their bodies, forcing her slightly away from him so that he could cup the soft weight of them. Just remembering that moment now was enough to bring back an unwanted echo of the sensation of his own desire, roaring through his body as an unstoppable force. It hadn't been enough to flick his tongue-tip against each hardened nipple and feel it quivering under its soft lash. Nothing had been enough until he had drawn the swollen flesh into his mouth, enticing its increased response with the delicate grate of his teeth.

He had heard Ruby cry out and felt her shudder. His hands had been swift to dispose of her skirt so that he could slide his hands into her unexpectedly respectable plain white knickers, to hold and knead the soft flesh of her buttocks. Swollen and stiff with the ferocity of his anger-induced arousal, he had lifted her onto the bed, plundering the softness of her plum painted mouth in between removing his own clothes, driven by the heat of his frustration against his grandfather, not caring about the girl whose body was underneath him, only knowing that within it he could find release.

Ruby had wrapped her arms round him whilst he had plundered her mouth, burying her face in his shoulder once he was naked, pretending to be too shy to look at him, never mind touch him. But he hadn't been interested in playing games. To him she had simply been a means to an end. And as for her touching him… Sander tensed his muscles against his remembered awareness of exactly what her intimate touch on him would have precipitated. His body had been in no mood to wait and in no condition to need stimulus or further arousal. That alone was something he would have claimed impossible prior to that night. No other situation had ever driven him to such a peak of erotic immediacy.

No other situation or no other woman? Grimly Sander tried to block the unwanted question. His subconscious had no business raising such an unnecessary suggestion. He didn't want to probe any further into the past. But even though he pulled the laptop back towards himself and opened his e-mails, he still couldn't concentrate on them. His mind was refusing to co-operate, returning instead to its memories. Against his will more old images Ruby began to surface, refusing to be ignored. He was back in that hotel bedroom in Manchester. Sander closed his eyes and gave in.

In the dim light Ruby's body had been alabaster-pale, her skin flawless and her body delicately female. The lamplight had thrown a shadow from the soft mound of flesh covered by her knickers, which he had swiftly removed. That, he remembered, had caused him to glance up at the tangled mass of hair surrounding her face, surprised to discover that the colour of her hair was natural. Somehow the fact that she was naturally blonde didn't go with the image she had created, with her thick make-up and tight, clinging clothes.

She had met his look and then looked away, the colour coming and going in her face as her glance rested on his body and then skittered away.

If her naturally blonde hair had been at odds with his assessment of her, then her breathy voice, unsteady and on the verge of awed apprehension, had been enough to fill him with contempt.

'You look very big,' she had delivered, within a heartbeat of her glance skittering away from his erection.

Had she really thought him both foolish and vain enough to be taken in by a ploy like that? If so he had made sure that she knew that he wasn't by taunting her deliberately, parting her legs with his hand.

'But not bigger than any of the others, I'm sure.'

She had said something—a few gasped words—but he hadn't been listening by then. He had been too busy exploring the wet eagerness of her sex, stroking his fingertip its length until he reached the hard pulse of her clitoris, and by that stage she had begun to move against his touch and moan softly at the same time, in a rising crescendo of excitement.

He had told himself that her supposed arousal was almost bound to be partly faked but unexpectedly his body had responded to it as though it was real. It had increased his own urgency, so that he had replaced his fingers with the deliberate thrust of his sex. She had tensed then, looking up at him with widened dark eyes that had filled with fake tears when he had thrust properly into her, urged by the wanton tightness of her muscles as they clung to him, as though wanting to hold and possess him. Their resistance had incited him to drive deeper and deeper into her, just for the pleasure of feeling their velvet clasp. He had come quickly and hotly, his lack of control catching him off-guard, her body tightening around him as he pulsed into her.

Sander wrenched his thoughts back to the present. What had happened with Ruby was not an interlude in his life or an aspect of himself that reflected well on him, he was forced to admit. In fact part of the reason he had chosen to lock these memories away in the first place had been because of his sense of angry distaste. Like something rotten, they carried with them the mental equivalent of a bad odour that couldn't be ignored or masked. If he judged Ruby harshly for her part in their encounter, then he judged himself even more harshly—especially now that he knew the consequences of those few out of control seconds of raw male sensuality.

It was because he didn't like the fact that his sons had been conceived in such a way that he was experiencing the regrets he was having now, Sander told himself. He owed them a better beginning to their life than that.

What was it that was gnawing at him now? Regret because his sons had been conceived so carelessly, so uncaringly, and in anger? Or something more than that? Regret that he hadn't taken more time to—? To what? To get to know the mother of his sons better or to think of the consequences of his actions? Because deep down inside he felt guilty about the way he had treated Ruby? She had only been seventeen after all.

He hadn't known that then, Sander defended himself. He had assumed she was much older. And if he had known…?

Sander stood up and paced the floor of his office, stopping abruptly as he relived how, virtually as soon as he had released her, Ruby had gone to the bathroom. He had turned on his side, ignoring her absence, even then aware of how far his behaviour had fallen short of his own normal high standards. But even though he had wanted to blot out the reality of the situation, and Ruby herself, he had still somehow been unable to stop listening to the sound of the shower running and then ceasing, had been aware against his will of her return to the bed, her skin cold and slightly damp as she pressed up against his back, shivering slightly. He had had no need for intimacy with her any more. She had served her purpose, and he preferred sleeping alone. And yet for some reason, despite all of that, he had turned over and taken her in his arms, feeling her body stiffen and then relax as he held her.

She had fallen asleep with her head on his chest, murmuring in protest in her sleep every time he tried to ease away from her, so that he had spent the night with her cuddled up against him. And wasn't it true that somehow she had done something to him during those night hours? Impressed herself against his body and his senses so that once in a while over the years that had followed he would wake up from a deep sleep, expecting to find her there lying against him and feeling as though a part of him was missing because she wasn't?

How long had he fought off that admission, denying its existence, pretending to himself that since he had returned to the island this time his sleep had never once been disturbed by that aching absence? He moved impatiently towards the window, opening it to breathe in fresh air in an attempt to clear his head.

What had brought all this on? Surely not a simple comment from Anna that she considered Ruby to be a good mother. A good mother *and* a good wife, he reminded himself.

His mobile had started to ring. He reached for it, frowning when he saw his sister's name flash up on the screen.

'Sander, we've been back from America nearly a week now. When are you going to bring Ruby to Athens so that I can meet her?'

Elena liked to talk, and it was several minutes before Sander could end the call, having agreed that, since he was due to pay one of his regular visits to the Athens office anyway, he would take Ruby with him so that she and Elena could meet.

CHAPTER TEN

SHE had better find out for sure that she was pregnant, and if so tell Sander. She couldn't put it off much longer, Ruby warned herself. She wasn't the only one to blame after all. It took two, and she *had* taken her birth control pills.

She had also been unwell, she reminded herself, and in the anxiety and despair of everything that had been happening in London she had forgotten that that could undermine the effectiveness of the pills. Surely Sander would be able to understand that? But what if he didn't? What if he accused her of deliberately flouting his wishes? But what possible reason could she logically have for doing that? He was a successful, intelligent businessman. He would be bound to recognise that there was no logical reason for her to deliberately allow herself to become pregnant. He might be a successful, intelligent businessman, but he had also been a child whose mother had betrayed him. Would *that* have any bearing on the fact that she was pregnant? On the face of it, no—but Ruby had an instinctive feeling that it might.

She would tell him tonight, Ruby promised herself, once the boys were in bed.

Her mind made up, Ruby was just starting to relax when Sander himself appeared, striding from the house onto the patio area, quite plainly in search of her. Her heart somersaulted with guilt. Had he somehow guessed? At least if he had then her pregnancy would be out in the open and they could discuss it rationally. It was only when he told her that his sister had been on the phone, and that they would be leaving for Athens in morning and staying there for the night, that Ruby realised, cravenly, that a part of her had actually hoped that he *had* guessed, and that she would be spared the responsibility of telling him that she had once again conceived.

Since he hadn't guessed, though, it was sensible, surely, to wait until they returned from Athens to tell him? That way they would have more time to discuss the issue properly. He would be angry, she knew that, but she was clinging to the knowledge that he loved the twins, and using that knowledge to reassure herself that, angry though he would no doubt be with her, he would love this new baby as well.

'I've got a small apartment in Athens that I use when I'm there on business. We'll stay there. The twins will be safe and well looked after here, with Anna.'

'Leave them behind?' Ruby checked. 'They haven't spent a single night without me since they were born.'

Her anxious declaration couldn't possibly be fake, Sander recognised. It had been too immediate and automatic for that. He tried to imagine his own mother refusing a trip to a cosmopolitan city filled with expensive designer shops to stay with her children, and acknowledged that it would never have happened. His mother had hated living on the island, had visited it as infrequently as she could, and he himself had been sent to boarding school in England as soon as he had reached his seventh birthday.

'Elena will want to spend time with you, and I have business matters to attend to. The boys will be far happier here on the island in Anna's care than they would be in a city like Athens.'

When Ruby bit her lip, her eyes still shadowed, he continued, 'I can assure you that you can trust Anna to look after them properly. If I did not believe that myself, there would be no question of us leaving them.'

Immediately Ruby's gaze cleared.

'Oh, I know I can trust your judgement when it comes to their welfare. I know how much you love them.'

Her immediate and open admission that she accepted not only his judgement for their sons but with it his right to make such a judgement was having the most extraordinary effect on him, Sander realised. Like bright sunlight piercing a hitherto dark and impenetrable black cloud. He was bemused and dazzled by the sudden surge of pleasure her words gave him— the feeling that they were united, and that she…that she *trusted* him, Sander recognised. Ruby trusted him to make the right decision for their sons. A surge of unfamiliar emotion swamped him, and he had an alien and overpowering urge to take her in his arms and hold her tight. He took a step towards her, and then stopped as his need to protect himself cut in.

Unaware of Sander's reaction to her statement, Ruby sighed. She was being silly, she knew. The twins *would* be perfectly safe with Anna. Was it really for their sakes she wanted them with her? Or was it because she felt their presence was a form of protection and was nervous at the thought of meeting Sander's sister? Had they had a normal marriage she would have been able to admit her apprehension to Sander—but then if they were in a normal marriage she would already have told him about the new baby, and that news would have been a matter of joy and happiness for both of them.

'You will like Elena—although, as I told her often when she was a little girl, she talks all the time and sometimes forgets to let others speak.' Anna shook her head as she relayed this information to Ruby. She was helping her to pack for the trip to Athens—her offer, Ruby suspected, more because she had sensed her trepidation and wanted to reassure her than because she really felt Ruby needed help.

'She is very proud of her brothers, especially Sander, and she will be glad that he has married you when she sees how much you love him.'

Ruby dropped the pair of shoes she had been holding, glad that the act of bending down to pick them up gave her an opportunity to hide her shock. How much she loved Sander? What on earth had made Anna think and say that? She didn't love him at all.

Did she?

Of course not. After all, he hadn't exactly given her any reason to love him, had he?

Since when had love needed a reason? What reason had she needed in that Manchester club, when she had looked across the bar and felt her heart leap inside her chest, as though he himself had tugged it and her towards him?

That had been the silly, naive reaction of a girl desperate to create a fairytale hero—a saviour to rescue her from her grief, Ruby told herself, beginning to panic.

Anna was mistaken. She had to be. But when she had recovered her composure enough to look at the other woman she saw from the warm compassion in her eyes that Anna herself certainly didn't think that she was wrong.

Was it possible? *Could* she have started to

love Sander without realising it? Could the aching, overwhelming physical desire for him she could not subdue be caused by love and not merely physical need? He was, after all, the father of her children, and she couldn't deny that initially when she had realised that she was pregnant a part of her had believed she had conceived because of the intensity of her emotional response to him. Because she had been naive, and frightened and alone, she had wanted to believe that the twins had been created out of love.

And this new baby—didn't it too deserve to have its mother's body accept the seed that began its life with love?

'You will like Elena,' Anna repeated, 'and she will like you.'

Ruby was clinging to those words several hours later, after their plane had touched down in Athens and they were in the arrivals hall, as an extremely stylish dark-haired young woman came hurrying towards them, her eyes covered by a pair of designer sunglasses.

'Sander. I thought I was going to be late. The traffic is horrendous—and the smog! No wonder all our precious ancient buildings are in so much danger. Andreas said to tell you that he is pretty sure he has secured the Taiwan contract—oh, and I want you both to come to dinner tonight. Nothing too formal…'

'Elena, you are like a runaway train. Stop and let me introduce you to Ruby.' Sander's tone was firm but wry, causing his sister to laugh and then turn to Ruby, catching her off-guard when she immediately enveloped her in a warm hug.

'Anna has told me what a fortunate man Sander is to have married you. I can't wait to meet the twins. Wasn't I clever, spotting them at Manchester Airport? But for me you and Sander might never have made up your quarrel and been reconciled.'

They were out of the airport now, and Sander was saying, 'You'd better let me drive,

Elena. I have some expensive memories of what happens when you drive and talk at the same time.'

'Oh, you.' Elena mock pouted as she handed over her car keys, and then told Ruby, 'It wasn't really my fault. The other driver should never have been parked where he was in the first place.'

Anna was right—she was going to like Elena, Ruby acknowledged as her sister-in-law kept up a stream of inconsequential chatter and banter whilst Sander drove them through the heavy Athens traffic.

Elena had obviously questioned Sander about their relationship, and from what she had said Ruby suspected that he had made it seem as though the twins had been conceived during an established relationship between them rather than a one-night stand. That had been kind of him. Kind and thoughtful. Protecting the twins and protecting her. The warm glow she could feel inside herself couldn't possibly be happiness, could it?

* * *

The Athens night was warm, the soft air stroking Ruby's skin as she and Sander walked from the taxi that had just dropped them off to the entrance to the exclusive modern building that housed Sander's Athens apartment. They had spent the evening with Elena and Andreas at their house on the outskirts of the city, and tomorrow morning they would be returning to the island. Of course she was looking forward to seeing the twins, but… Was she simply deceiving herself, because it was what she wanted, or had there really been a softening in Sander's attitude towards her today? A kindness and a warmth that had made her feel as though she was poised on the brink of something special and wonderful?

Sander looked at Ruby. She was wearing a pale peach silk dress patterned with a design of pale grey fans. It had shoestring straps, a fitted bodice and a gently shaped slim skirt. Its gentle draping hinted at the feminine shape of her figure without revealing too much of it, and the strappy bodice revealed the tan her skin had acquired in the weeks she had spent on the island. Tonight, watching her over dinner as she had talked and smiled and laughed with his sister and her husband, he had felt pride in her as his wife, as well as desire for her as a man. Something—Sander wasn't prepared to give it a name—had begun to change. Somehow *he* had begun to change. Because Ruby was a good mother? Because she had trusted him about the twins' care? Because tonight she had shown an intelligence, a gentleness and a sense of humour that—a little to his own surprise— he had recognised were uniquely hers, setting her apart from his mother and every other woman he had known?

Sander wasn't ready to answer those questions, but he was ready and eager to make love to his wife.

To make love to her *as* his wife. A simple enough statement, but for Sander it resonated with admissions that he would have derided as impossible the day he had married her.

As they entered the apartment building Sander reached for Ruby's hand. Neither of them said anything, but Ruby's heart leapt and then thudded into the side of her chest. The hope she had been trying desperately not to let go to her head was now soaring like a helium balloon.

On the way up to the apartment in the lift she pleaded mentally, 'Please let everything be all right. Please let things work out for…for *all* of us.' And by all she included the new life she was carrying as well.

She *was* going to tell Sander, but today whilst she had had the chance she had slipped into a chemist's shop and bought a pregnancy testing kit—just to be doubly sure. She would wait until they were back on the island to use it, and then she *would* tell Sander. Then, but not now. Because she wanted tonight to be very special. Tonight she wanted for herself. Tonight she wanted to make love with Sander, knowing that she loved him.

* * *

In the small sitting room of the apartment, Sander removed the jacket of his linen suit, dropping it onto one of the chairs. The small action tightened the fabric of his shirt against the muscles of his back, and Ruby's gaze absorbed their movement, the now familiar ache of longing softening her belly and then spreading swiftly through her. Her sudden need to breathe more deeply, to take in oxygen, lifted her breasts against the lining of her dress, causing her already aroused and sensitive nipples to react even more to the unintentional drag of the fabric. When Sander straightened up and turned round he could see their swollen outline pressing eagerly against the barrier of her dress. His own body reacted to their provocation immediately, confirming the need for her he had already known he felt.

She couldn't stand here like this, Ruby warned herself. If she did Sander was bound to think she was doing so because she wanted him and was all too likely to say so. She didn't want that. She didn't want to be accused of being a woman who could not live without sexual satisfaction. What she wanted was to be told that he couldn't resist her, that he adored her and loved her.

Quickly Ruby turned towards the door, not wanting Sander to see her expression, but to her astonishment before she could reach it he said quietly, 'You looked beautiful tonight in that dress.'

Sander was telling her she looked beautiful?

Ruby couldn't move. She couldn't do anything other than stare at him, torn between longing and disbelief.

Sander was coming towards her, standing in front of her, lifting his hands to slide the straps of her dress off her shoulders as he told her softly, 'But you will look even more beautiful without it.'

The words were nothing, and yet at the same time they were everything. Ruby trembled from head to foot, hardly daring to breathe as Sander unzipped her dress so that it could fall to the floor and then cupped the side of her face and kissed her.

She was in Sander's arms, and he was kissing her, and she was kissing him back. Kissing him back, holding him, feeling all her doubts and fears slipping away from her like sand sucked away by the sea as her love for him claimed her.

The sensation of Sander's hands on her body, shaping it and caressing it, carried her on a surging tide of her own desire, like a tribute offered to an all powerful conqueror. His lightest touch made her body shudder softly in swiftly building paroxysms of pleasure. She had hungered to have him desire her like this, without the harsh bitterness of his anger. In the deepest hidden places of her heart Ruby recognised that, even if she had hidden that need from herself. She had hungered, ached, and denied that aching—yearned for him and forbidden that yearning. But now, here tonight in his arms, the lies she had told to protect herself were melting away, burned away by the heat of his hands on her body, leaping from nerve-ending to nerve-ending. Beneath Sander's mouth Ruby moaned in heightened pleasure when his thumb-pad rubbed over her nipple, hot, sweet and aching need pulsing beneath his touch. Her body was clamouring for him to free it, to lay it bare to his eyes, his hands, his mouth, so that he could plunder its desire, feed it and feast on it, until she could endure the ache of her own need no longer and she clung to him whilst he took her to the heights and the final explosion that would give him all that she was and all that she had to give, make her helpless under the power of his possession and her own need for it, for him.

This was how it had been that first night in Manchester, with her senses overwhelmed by the intensity of what she was experiencing. So much so, in fact, that she had scarcely noticed the loss of her virginity. She'd been so desperate for his possession and for the pleasure it had brought her.

She was his, and Sander allowed himself to

glory in that primeval knowledge. His body was on fire for her, aching beyond bearing with his need for her, but he wanted to draw out their pleasure—to savour it and store the unique bouquet of it in his memory for ever. He bent and picked her up, carrying her through into the bedroom, their gazes meeting and locking in the sensually charged warmth of the dimly lit room.

'I've never forgotten you—do you know that? I've never been able to get your memory out of my head. The way you trembled against me when I touched you, the scent of your skin, the quick, unsteady way you breathed when I did this.'

Ruby fought to suppress her breathing now, as Sander caressed the side of her neck and then stroked his fingertips the length of her naked spine.

'Yes, just like that.'

Helplessly Ruby whimpered against the lash of her own pleasure, protesting that Sander was tormenting her and she couldn't bear any more, but Sander ignored her, tracing a line of kisses along her shoulderblade. When he had done that the first time she had arched her back in open delight, helpless against the onslaught of her own desire. Sander lifted her arm and began kissing the inside of her wrist and then the inside of her elbow. He had never known that it was possible for him to feel like this, Sander acknowledged. The sensual sweetness of Ruby's response to him was crashing through all the defences he had raised against the way she was making him feel.

He kissed her mouth, probing its soft, welcoming warmth with his tongue, whilst Ruby trembled against him, her naked body arching up to his, the feel of her skin through his clothes a torment he could hardly bear.

Ruby was lost beneath the hot, intimate possession of Sander's kiss—a kiss that was sending fiery darts of arousal and need rushing through her body to turn the existing dull ache low down within it into an open pulsing need.

Her breasts yearned for his touch, her nipples throbbing and swollen like fruit so ripe their readiness could hardly be contained within their skin. She wanted to feel his hands on her body, stroking, caressing, satisfying her growing need. Wanted his lips kissing and sucking the ache from her breasts and transforming it to the liquid heat of pleasure. But instead he was pulling away from her, lifting his body from hers, abandoning her when she needed him so desperately. Frantically Ruby shook her head, her protest an inarticulate soft moan as she sat up in the bed.

As though he knew how she felt, and what she feared, Sander reached for her hand and carried it to his own body, laying it flat against the hard swell of his flesh under the fabric of his suit trousers, his gaze never leaving her face as it registered her passion stoked delight in his erection, and its sensual underlining of his own desire for her.

Very slowly her fingertips traced the length

and thickness of his flesh, everything she was feeling visible to him in the soft parting of her mouth, the brief flick of her tongue-tip against her lips and the excitement darkening her absorbed gaze.

Impatiently Sander started to unfasten his shirt. Distracted by his movements, Ruby looked up at him and then moved closer, kneeling on the bed in front of him as she took over the task from him. She leaned forward to kiss the flesh each unfastened button exposed, and then gave in to the impulse driving her to know more than the warmth of his skin against her lips, stroking her tongue-tip along his breastbone, breathing in the pheromone-laden scent of his body as it shuddered beneath her caress. His chest was hard-muscled, his nipples flat and dark. Lost in the heady pleasure of being so close to him, Ruby reached out and touched the hard flesh with her fingertip, and then on an impulse that came out of nowhere she bent her head and kissed the same spot, exploring it with the tip of her tongue.

Reaction ricocheted through Sander, engulfing and consuming him. He'd been unfastening his trousers whilst Ruby explored him, and now he wrenched off what was left of his clothes before taking Ruby in his arms to kiss her with the full force of his building need.

The sensation of Sander's body against her, with no barriers between them, swept away what were left of Ruby's inhibitions. Wrapping her arms around Sander's neck, she clung to him, returning his kiss with equal passion, sighing her approval when his hands cupped her breasts.

This was what his heart had been yearning for, Sander admitted. This giving and receiving, this intimacy with no barriers, this woman above all women. Ruby was everything he wanted and more, Sander acknowledged, making his own slow voyage of rediscovery over Ruby's silk-soft body.

Sander prided himself on being a skilled lover, but he had never been in this position before. He had never felt like this before. He wasn't prepared for his own reaction to the way he felt. He wasn't prepared for the way it powered his own desire to a level he had never known before, threatening his self-control, creating within him a desire to possess and pleasure every part of her, to bring her to orgasm over and over again, until he possessed her pleasure and her with it. He wanted to imprint himself on her desire so that no other man could ever unlock its sweetness. He wanted *her*, Sander acknowledged, and he fed the fast-surging appetite of his own arousal on the sound of her unsteady breathing, interspersed with sobs of pleasure, as he sucked on the hard peaks of her nipples and kneaded the soft flesh of her breasts.

Ruby arched up towards him, her hands clasped on the back of his neck to hold him against her. She had thought that Sander had already taken her to the utmost peak of sensual pleasure, but she had been wrong. Now, with the barriers between them down, she knew that what had gone before had been a mere shadow of what she was feeling now. Lightning-fast bolts of almost unbearable erotic arousal sheeted through her body with every tug of Sander's mouth on her nipples, going to ground deep inside her, feeding the hot pulse already beating there, until merely arching up against him wasn't enough to appease the savage dragging need possessing her. Instead she had to open her legs and press herself against him, her breath catching on a grateful moan of relief when Sander responded to her need with the firm pressure of his hand over her sex.

Against his hand Sander could feel the heavy pulsing beat of Ruby's need. It drove the ache within his own flesh to a maddening desire to take her quickly and hotly, making him fight for the self-control that threatened to desert him when he parted the swollen outer lips of her sex to find the wetness within them.

It was almost more than Ruby could stand to have Sander touching her so intimately, and yet at the same time nowhere nearly intimately enough. His fingertip rimmed the opening to her sex. A fresh lightning bolt shot through her. She could feel her body opening to him in eagerness and hunger, heard a sound of agonised relief bubbling in her throat when Sander slid one and then two fingers slowly inside her.

He didn't need Ruby's fingers gripping his arm or her nails digging into his flesh to tell him what she was feeling. Sander could feel her need in his own flesh and hers as the movement of her body quickened and tightened. Even before she cried out to him he was aware of her release, and the quick, fierce pleasure of her orgasm filled his own body with fierce male satisfaction, swelling his sex to a hard urgency to play its part in more of that pleasure.

But not yet—not until he was sure that he had given her all the pleasure he could.

For Ruby, the sensation of Sander's lips caressing their way down her supine body was initially one of relaxed easy sweetness—a tender caress after the white-hot heat that had gone before it. She had no intimation, no warning of the fresh urgency to come, until Sander's lips drifted across her lower belly and the ache she had thought satisfied began to pulse and swell in a new surge of need that shocked her into an attempt to deny its existence.

But Sander wouldn't let her. Her protests were ignored, and the growing pleasure of her wanton flesh was cherished with hot swirls of desire painted on her inner thighs by the stroke of his tongue—a tongue that searched out her desire even more intimately, until its movement against the hard swollen pulse of her clitoris had her abandoning her self-control once more and offering herself up to him.

This time her orgasm was short and sharp,

leaving her trembling on the edge of something more. Agonised by the ache of that need, Ruby reached out to touch Sander's body, but he stopped her, shaking his head as he told her thickly, 'No. Don't. Let me do this instead.'

She could feel the glide of his body against her own, his sex hard and slick, probing the eager moistness of hers, and her muscles quickened in eager longing, matching each slow, deliberate ever deeper thrust of his body within her own.

Aaahhh—how she remembered the first time he had shown her this pleasure and revealed its mystery. The way it had taken her beyond that small sharp pain which had caught at her breath and held her motionless beneath his thrust for a handful of seconds before her arousal had made its own demands on her, her muscles softening to enfold him, just as they were doing now, then firming to caress him, her body driven by its need to have him ever deeper within her.

This was what her body had yearned and

hungered for—this completeness and whole-ness, beyond any other, as she clung to Sander, taking him fully within her and holding him there, welcoming and matching the growing speed of his rhythm.

He was lost, Sander recognised. His self-control, his inner self stripped away, taking from him his power to do anything other than submit to his own need as it rolled over him and picked him up with its unstoppable force.

He heard himself cry out, a male sound of mingled agony and triumph, as Ruby's fresh orgasm took them both over the edge, his body flooding hers with his own release.

Her body still racked by small aftershocks of the seismic pleasure that had erupted inside her, Ruby lay silently against Sander's chest, heard their racing heartbeats gradually slowing.

Tonight they had shared something special, something precious, Ruby thought, and her heart overflowed with love.

CHAPTER ELEVEN

THE twins' matter-of-fact response to their return to the island proved more than any amount of words how comfortable they had been in Anna's care during her absence, Ruby reflected ruefully in her bedroom, as she changed out of the clothes she had travelled home in. Sander had gone straight to his office to check his e-mails.

But getting changed wasn't all she needed to do.

Her handbag was on the bed. She opened it and removed the pregnancy testing kit she had bought in Athens. Her hands trembled slightly as she took it from its packaging, her eyes blurring with emotion as she read the instructions. Six years ago when she had done this she had been so afraid, sick with fear, dreading the result.

She was equally anxious now, but for very different reasons.

Things had changed since she had first realised that she might be pregnant again, she tried to reassure herself. When Anna had referred to her love for Sander, initially Ruby had wanted to deny it. But once that truth had been laid bare for her to see she hadn't been able to ignore it. Of *course* she loved Sander. The real shock was that she hadn't realised that for herself but had needed Anna to tell her. Now, just thinking about him filled her with aching longing and pain.

Maybe this baby would build the bridge between them, if she lowered her own pride and told him how she felt. She had begged him to give her the possession of his body—would it really be so very difficult to plead with him to accept her love? To plead with him that this child might be born into happiness and the love of both its parents? He loved the twins—surely he would love this child as well, even if he refused to accept her love for him? Telling herself that she must have faith that the love she had seen Sander give the twins would not be reserved for the twins alone, she walked towards the bathroom.

Ten minutes later Ruby was still standing in the bathroom, her gaze fixed on the telltale line. She had known, of course—impossible for her not to have done. But nothing was the same as visible confirmation. Against Sander's explicit wishes she had conceived his child. Ruby thought of the contraceptive pills she had taken so carefully and regularly every evening, in obedience to Sander's conditions for their marriage. Perhaps this baby, conceived against all the odds, was meant to be—a gift to them both that they could share together? She put her hand on her still flat body and took a deep breath. She would have to tell Sander now, and the sooner the better.

The sudden childish scream of anger she could hear from outside had her letting the test fall onto the marble surface surrounding the hand basin as she ran to the patio doors in the bedroom in automatic response to the outraged sound. Outside on the patio, as she had expected, she found the twins quarrelling over a toy. Freddie was attempting to drag it away from Harry, whilst Harry wailed in protest. Anna, alerted as Ruby had been by the noise, wasn't far behind her, and the two of them quickly defused the situation.

Once they had done so, Anna said matter-of-factly, 'You will have your hands full if it is twins again that you are carrying.'

Ruby shook her head. She wasn't really surprised that Anna had guessed. The homemade ginger biscuits that had discreetly begun to appear with her morning cup of weak tea had already hinted to her that Anna shared her own suspicions.

Sander pushed back his chair. They had only arrived at the villa an hour ago, and yet already he was conscious of an urge to seek out Ruby, and with it an awareness that he was actually missing her company—and not just in bed. Such feelings made him feel vulnerable, something that Sander instinctively resisted and resented, and yet at the same time he was opening his office door and striding down the corridor in the direction of their bedroom.

Ruby would be outside with the twins. As their father, he could legitimately get changed and go and join them. Doing so would not betray him. And if he was there as much so that he could be with Ruby as with his sons, then only he needed to know that. The conditioning of a lifetime of fearing emotional betrayal could not be overturned in the space of a few short weeks. Others close to him, like Anna and Elena, might admire Ruby and think her a good wife, but Sander told himself that he needed more proof that he could trust her.

He noted the presence of Ruby's open handbag on their bed as he made his way to the bathroom, but it was only after he had showered and changed that he noticed the discarded pregnancy test.

The first thing Ruby saw when she went back into the bedroom was Sander's suit jacket on the bed. Her heart started to hammer too heavily and far too fast, with a mixture of guilt and fear. She walked towards the bathroom, coming to an abrupt halt when she saw Sander standing beside the basin, holding the telltale test.

There was a blank look in his eyes, as though he couldn't quite believe what he was seeing. A blank look that was soon burned away by the anger she could see replacing it as he looked at her.

'You're pregnant.'

It was an accusation, not a question, and Ruby's heart sank.

'Yes,' she admitted. 'I thought I might be, but I wanted to be sure before I told you. I know what you said when we got married about me taking the pill because you didn't want another child—and I did take it,' she told him truthfully. When he didn't say anything, but simply continued to look at her she was panicked into pleading emotionally, 'Please don't look at me like that. You love the twins, and this baby, *your* baby, deserves to be loved as well.'

'*My* child? Since you have said yourself that you were on the pill, it cannot possibly be my child. We both know that. Do you really think me such a fool that I would let you pass off a brat conceived with one of the no doubt many men who happened to be enjoying your body before I found you? If so, then you are the one who is a fool. But you are not a fool, are you, Ruby? You are a venal, lying, amoral and greedy woman.'

The words exploded into the room like randomly discharged machine gun fire, meant to destroy everything it hit. Right now she might be too numb to feel anything, but Ruby knew that she had been mortally wounded.

'You obviously knew when you demanded that I marry you that you were carrying this child,' Sander accused her savagely.

He had claimed that he was not a fool, but the opposite was true. He had allowed her to tempt him out of the security of the emotional mindset he had grown up with and to believe that maybe—just maybe—he had been wrong about her. But of course he had not been. He deserved the punishment of what he was feeling now for dropping his guard, for deliberately ignoring all the safeguards he had put in place to protect himself. The bitter, angry thoughts raked Sander's pride with poison-dipped talons.

'I thought you had married me for the financial gain you believed you could get from our marriage, but I can see now that I didn't recognise the true depth of your greed and lack of morals.'

Ruby couldn't bear any more.

'I married you for the sake of our sons,' she

told him fiercely. 'And this child I am carrying now is yours. Yes, I took the pill, but if you remember I wasn't well whilst we were in London. I believe that is how I came to conceive. In some circumstances a…a stomach upset and nausea can damage the pill's efficiency.'

'A very convenient excuse,' Sander sneered. 'Do you *really* expect me to believe it, knowing you as I do? You didn't marry me for the twins' sake, Ruby. You married me for my money.'

'That's not true,' Ruby denied. How could he think so badly of her? Anger joined her pain. Sander had called himself a fool, but *she* was the fool. For loving him, and for believing that she could reach out to him with that love.

'I know you,' he repeated, and hearing those words Ruby felt her self-control break.

'No, you don't know me, Sander. All you know is your own blind prejudice. When this baby is born I shall have its DNA tested, and I can promise you now that he or she will be proved to be your child and a true sibling to the twins. However, by then it will be too late for you to know it and love it as your son or daughter, Sander, because there is no way I intend to allow my children to grow up with a father who feels and speaks as you do. You love the twins, I can see that, but as they grow to be men your attitude to me, their mother, your suspicions of me, are bound to contaminate their attitude to my sex. I will *not* have my sons growing up like you—unable to recognise love, unable to value it, unable to even see it.

'Do you know what my worst sin has been? The thing I regret the most? It's loving *you*, Sander. Because in loving you, I am not being a good mother to my children. You've constantly thrown at me my behaviour the first time we met, accusing me of being some wanton who came on to you. The truth is that I was a seventeen-year-old virgin—oh, yes you may look at me like that but it's true—a naive and recklessly silly girl who, in the aftermath of losing her parents, ached so much for love to replace what she had lost that she convinced herself a man she saw across a crowded bar was her saviour, a hero, someone special who would lift her up out of the misery of her pain and loss and hold her safe in his arms. That was the true nature of my crime, Sander—idolising you and turning you into something you could never be.

'And as for all those other men you like to accuse me of being with—they never existed. Not a single one of them. Do you *really* think I would be stupid enough to trust another man after the way you treated me? Yes, I expect I deserved it for behaving so stupidly. You wanted to teach me a lesson, I expect. I'm only surprised, knowing you as I now do, that you seem unable to accept that your lesson was successful.

'There was only one reason I asked you for marriage, Sander—because I thought it would make you back off. But then, when I realised you genuinely wanted the twins, it was as I told you at the time—because I believe very strongly that children thrive best emotionally within the security of a family unit that contains two parents who intend to stay together. I grew up in that kind of family unit, and naturally it was what I wanted for my sons.

'What you've just accused me of changes everything. I don't want you poisoning the boys' minds with your own horrible mindset. This baby *will* be their true sibling, but somehow I doubt that even DNA evidence will convince you of that. Quite simply it isn't what you want to believe. You want to believe the worst of me. Perhaps you even need to believe it. In which case I feel very sorry for you. My job as a mother is to protect all my children. The twins are two very intelligent boys. They will quickly see that you do not accept their sister or brother and they might even mimic your behaviour. I will not allow that to happen.'

Initially he had been resolutely determined to deny that there could be any truth in Ruby's angry outburst. But beneath the complex defence system his own hurt emotions had built up to protect him from the pain caused by his mother, tendrils of something 'other' had begun to unfurl. So small at first that he thought he could brush them away. But when he tried Sander discovered that they were rooted in a bedrock of inner need it stunned him to discover. When had this yearning to throw off the defensive chains that imprisoned him taken root? How could this part of him actually be willing to take Ruby's side against himself? Struggling against the opposing forces within himself, Sander fought desperately for a way forward.

This was so much worse than anything she had imagined might happen, Ruby acknowledged. She had feared that Sander would be angry, but it had never occurred to her that he would refuse to accept that the child she had conceived was his. She should hate him for that. She wished that she could. Hatred would be cleansing and almost satisfying.

She would have to leave the island, of

course. But she wasn't going anywhere without the twins. They would miss Sander dreadfully, but she couldn't risk them starting to think and feel as he did. She couldn't let his bitterness infect them.

She turned to look through the still open patio doors, her vision blurred by the tears she was determined not to let him see.

'There's no point in us continuing this discussion,' she told him. 'Since it's obvious that you prefer to think the worst of me.'

Without waiting to see if he was going to make any response Ruby headed for the patio, anxious to put as much distance between them as she could before her emotions overwhelmed her and the tears burning the backs of her eyes fell.

From the bedroom Sander watched her, his thoughts still at war with themselves. Ruby had reached the top of the flight of marble steps that led down to the lower part of the garden.

Blinking fiercely to hold back her tears, Ruby stepped forward, somehow mistiming her step, so that the heel of her shoe caught on the top step, pitching her forward.

Sander saw her stumble and then fall, tumbling down the marble steps. He raced after her, taking the steps two at a time to reach her crumpled body where it lay still at the bottom of the first flight of steps.

She was conscious—just. And her two words to him as he kneeled over her were agonized. 'My baby…'

CHAPTER TWELVE

'SHE'S coming round now. Ruby, can you hear us?'

Her clouded vision slowly cleared and the vague outlines of white-clad figures formed into two nurses and a doctor, all three of them smiling reassuringly at her. Hospital. She was in hospital? Automatically she began to panic.

'It's all right, Ruby. You had a nasty fall, but you're all right now. We've had to keep you sedated for a few days, to give your body time to rest, and we've performed some tests, so you're bound to feel woozy and confused. Just relax.'

Relax! Ruby put her hand on top of the flat white sheet pulled tightly over her body. She was attached to some kind of drip, she realised.

'My baby?' she demanded anxiously.

The nurse closest to her looked at the doctor. She'd lost her baby. Her fall—she remembered it now—had killed her baby. The pain was all-encompassing. She had let her baby down. She hadn't protected it properly, either from her fall or from its father's rejection. She felt too numb with grief to cry.

The nurse patted her hand. The doctor smiled at her.

'Your baby is fine, Ruby.'

She looked at them both in disbelief.

'You're just telling me that, aren't you? I've lost the baby really, haven't I?'

The doctor looked back at the nurse. 'I think we should let Ruby have a look for herself.' Turning to Ruby, he told her, 'The nurse will take you for a scan, Ruby, and then you will be able to see for yourself that your baby is perfectly well. Which is more than I will be able to say for you, if you continue to upset yourself.'

An hour later Ruby was back in her hospital

room, still gazing in awed delight at the image she'd been given—an image which showed quite clearly that her baby was indeed safe.

'You and your baby have both been very lucky,' the nurse told her when she came in a few minutes later to check up on her. 'You sustained a nasty head injury, and when you were taken into hospital on Theopolis they feared that a blood clot had developed. It meant they would have to terminate your pregnancy. Your husband refused to give his consent. He arranged for you to be brought here to this hospital in Athens, and for a specialist to be brought from America to treat you. Your husband said that you would never forgive him and he would never forgive himself if your pregnancy had to be terminated.'

Sander had said that? Ruby didn't know what to think.

'I dare say he will be here soon,' the nurse continued. 'Initially he insisted on staying here in the hospital with you, but Professor

Smythson told him to go home and get some rest once you were in the clear.'

As though on cue the door to her room opened and Sander was standing there. Discreetly the nurse whisked herself out of the room, leaving them alone together.

'The twins…' Ruby began anxiously.

'They know that you had a fall and that you had to come to hospital to be "mended". They're missing you, of course, but Anna is doing her best to keep them occupied.'

'The nurse was just telling me that it's thanks to you I still have my baby.'

'Our baby,' Sander corrected her quietly.

Ruby didn't know what to say—or think—so her emotions did both for her. Tears slid down her face.

'Ruby, don't,' Sander begged, leaving the foot of her bed, where he had been standing, to come and take hold of her hand, now disconnected from the drip she had been on as she no longer needed it. 'When I saw you falling down those steps I knew that no matter what I'd said, or what I thought I'd believed, the truth was that I loved you. I think I knew it that last night we spent in Athens, but I told myself that letting go of my doubts about you must be a slow and measured process. It took the realisation that I might have lost you to show me the truth. I deliberately blinded myself to what was real, just as you said. I wanted and needed to believe the very worst of you, and because of that—because of my fear of loving you and my pride in that fear—you and our child almost lost your lives.'

'My fall was an accident.'

'An accident that resulted from my blind refusal to accept what you were trying to tell me. Can you forgive me?'

'I love you, Sander. You know that. What I want now is for you to forgive yourself.' Ruby looked up at him. 'And not just forgive yourself about me.' Did she dare to say what she wanted to say? If she didn't seize this opportunity to do so she would regret it, Ruby warned herself, for Sander's sake more than for her own.

'I know your mother hurt you, Sander.'

'My mother never loved any of us. We were a duty she had to bear—literally as well as figuratively. My brother and sister and myself were the price she paid for my father's wealth, and for living the life she really wanted—a life of shallow, gaudy excess, lived in luxury at someone else's expense. The only time we saw her was when she wanted my father to give her more money. There was no room in her heart for us, no desire to make room there for us.'

Ruby's heart ached with compassion for him.

'It wasn't your fault that she rejected you, Sander. The flaw was within her, not you.'

His grip on her hand tightened convulsively.

'I guess I've always been distrustful of women—probably as a result of my relation-ship with my mother. When I saw you in that club I saw you in my mother's image. I didn't want to look beneath the surface. I believe now that a part of me did recognise how innocent and vulnerable you really were, but I was determined to reject it. I used you as a means of expressing my anger against my grandfather. My behaviour was unforgivable.'

'No.' Ruby shook her head. 'Under the circumstances it was predictable. Had I been the experienced party girl you thought, I suspect I would have known that something more than desire was driving you. We both made mistakes, Sander, but that doesn't mean we can't forgive ourselves and put them behind us. We were both defensive when we got married. You because of your mother, and me because I was ashamed of the way I'd behaved with you—giving away my virginity to a man who couldn't wait to throw me out of his bed and his life once he had had what he wanted.'

'Don't…' Sander groaned remorsefully. 'I'm sorry I said what I did about this new baby, Ruby. When you fell just before you lost consciousness you whispered to me—"my baby"—and I knew then that no matter what I had said, or thought I believed, the child inside you was mine, that it was impossible for it to have been fathered by anyone else. Can we start again? Can you still love me after the way I've behaved?'

In answer to his question Ruby lifted herself up off her pillows and kissed him gently, before telling him, 'It would be impossible for me not to love you, Sander.'

It was just over a month since Ruby, fully recovered from her fall, had returned to the island, and each day her happiness grew. Or so it seemed to her. Sander had already proved to her that he was a loving father to the twins, and now, in addition to proving to her that he intended to be an equally good father to the child she was carrying, he had also dedicated himself to proving to her that he was a wonderfully loving husband.

Lying next to him in their bed, Ruby felt her

heart swell with joy and love. Smiling in the darkness, she turned toward Sander, pressing a loving kiss against his chin.

'You know what will happen if you keep on doing that,' he warned her mock-seriously.

Ruby laughed. 'I thought I was the one who was unable to resist you, not the other way round,' she teased as she nestled closer to him, the soft curves of her naked body a sweet, warm temptation against his own.

'Does it feel like I'm able to resist you?' Sander asked her.

His hands were already stroking her skin; his breath was warm against her lips. Eagerly Ruby moved closer to him. It was still the same—that heart-stopping feeling of anticipation and longing that filled her when she knew he was going to kiss her.

'I love you...'

The words were breathed against her ear and then repeated against her lips, before Sander finally slowly stroked his tongue-tip against them deliberately, until Ruby couldn't wait any longer and placed her hands either side of his head. Her lips parted, a little shudder of longing rippling through her.

The sound of the accelerated speed of their breathing mingled with the movement of flesh against fabric, soft whispering sounds of sensuality and expectant desire.

As always, the sweetness of Ruby's arousal increased Sander's own desire. She showed her love for him so naturally and openly, with her desire whispered in soft words of love and longing, and encouragement and promises filling the air, breathed against his skin in an erotic litany of emotion. He could now admit that part of him had responded to that in her from the very start, and had in turn loved her for it, even if he had barricaded that knowledge away from himself.

The shape of her body was changing now, and her pregnancy was a gentle swell that he caressed gently before he kissed her growing bump.

Looking down at his dark head, Ruby stroked the smooth flesh at the nape of his neck. She knew now how much both she and this new baby meant to him.

Lying down beside her, Sander cupped her breast, allowing his lips to tease her nipple provocatively, his fingertips drifting tormentingly across her lower belly in a caress he knew she loved. Ruby closed her eyes and clung to him, riding the wave of her own desire as it swelled and pulsed inside her, smiling at the now familiar torment of building pleasure, of raw, sensual need that Sander knew exactly how to stretch out until it became almost unbearable.

Sander knew that if he placed his hand over her mound now he would be able to feel the insistent pulse it covered—just as he knew that the unsteady increase in her breathing meant that the stroke of his fingers within her would bring her almost immediately to orgasm, and that after that orgasm he would re-ignite her desire so that he could satisfy them both with the thrust of his body within hers. He could feel his self-control starting to give way.

His hand moved further down her body. The soft, scented wetness of her sex and the way she offered it to him with such sensual generosity turned his heart over inside his chest. He looked up at her as he parted the folded outer lips. A shudder ripped through her eyes, dark and wild with need. His fingertips stroked slowly through her wetness and then back again, to rub against the source of her desire, hard and swollen beneath his touch, making his own body throb in increasingly insistent demand. His lips caressed her nipple more urgently, his gaze registering the flush staining her skin and the growing intensity of the small shudders gripping her body.

'San—der…'

It was the way she said his name that did it— a soft plea of longing plaited with a tormenting thread of enticement that smashed through what was left of his self-control.

Ruby shuddered wildly beneath the sensation of Sander's mouth on her skin—her breasts, her belly, her thighs, and then finally her sex, where his tongue-tip stroked and probed and possessed until the pleasure made her gasp and then cry out.

Sander couldn't wait any longer. As it was he had to fight against himself to draw out their shared pleasure instead of giving in to the demand of his own flesh and its need to lose itself within her, holding them both on the rack of their shared longing before finally thrusting slowly into her, letting the responsive muscles of her body take him and possess him until they were riding the pleasure together to the ecstasy of shared love and release.

'I love you.'

'I love you.'

'You are my life, my world, light in my darkness, my Ruby beyond price.'

Held safe in Sander's arms, Ruby closed her

eyes, knowing that when she woke in the morning and for every morning, of their lives together, she would wake up held safe and loved.

EPILOGUE

'OH, RUBY, she's beautiful.'

Smiling proudly, Ruby looked on as her sisters admired their new niece, who was now just over one month old.

It had been a wonderful surprise when Sander had told her that he had arranged for her sisters and their husbands to visit the island, and Ruby thought it the best present he could have given her—barring, of course, his love and their new daughter.

'She's the image of Sander,' Lizzie announced, with an eldest sister authority that Ruby had no desire to refute.

After all, it was true that Hebe was the image of her father and her twin brothers, and, whilst

Sander had said prior to her birth that if they had a girl he would like her to look like her mother, Ruby rather thought that he didn't mind one little bit that she was a dark-haired, dark-eyed daddy's girl.

'It looks as though she can wind Sander and the boys round her little finger already.' Charlotte joined the conversation, adding ruefully, 'I'm itching to cuddle her properly, but this one—' she patted the bulge of her seven-month pregnancy ruefully '—obviously doesn't want me to. He kicked so hard when I tried.'

'Ah, so it *is* a boy, then.'

Ruby and Lizzie pounced in unison, laughing when their middle sister tried to protest and then glanced toward her husband, Raphael. He was standing with Sander, and Lizzie's husband Ilios, who was holding their two-month-old son Perry with the deftness of experienced fatherhood. The three men laughed and talked together.

'Well, yes, I think so from what I saw at the last scan!' she admitted ruefully. 'Of course I could be wrong, and the truth is that Raphael doesn't mind whether we have a boy or a girl, although personally…' She gave a small sigh and then said softly, 'I know it's silly, but I can't stop myself from imagining a little boy with Raphael's features.'

'It isn't silly at all,' Ruby immediately defended her. 'It's only natural. I love the fact that the twins and Hebe look like Sander.'

'I feel the same way about Perry,' Lizzie agreed, adding, 'That's what love does for you.'

Automatically they all turned to watch their husbands. 'It's lovely that our three babies will be so close in age—especially as the twins have one another,' Ruby added.

'Sander is so proud of the boys, Ruby. And proud of you, for the way you brought them up alone.'

'I wasn't alone,' Ruby objected, pointing out emotionally, 'They and I had both of you to support us and love us. I could never have managed without you.'

'And we would never have wanted you to—would we, Charlotte?' Lizzie told her.

'Never,' Charlotte agreed, squeezing Ruby's hand.

For a moment it was just the three of them again, sisters bonded together by the tragedy they had shared, and by their love and loyalty for one another, but then Charlotte broke the silence, enclosing them all to say softly, 'I think we must have some very special guardian angels watching over us.'

Once again they looked toward their husbands, before turning back to one another.

'We've certainly been lucky to meet and fall in love with such very special men,' Ruby said.

'And all the more special because they think *they* are the lucky ones in having met us.' Lizzie shook her head and then said ruefully, 'None of us could have imagined how things were going to turn out when I was worrying so much about having to go out to Thessalonica.'

The look she gave Ilios as she spoke said very

clearly to her sisters how much she loved her husband, causing both of them to turn and look at their own husbands with similar emotion.

'There is something other than how happy we are now that we do need to discuss,' she continued, explaining when Charlotte and Ruby looked at her, 'The house. Ilios insisted on clearing the mortgage for me, because at that stage I still thought that you would both need it, and I transferred it into your joint names. Since none of us need it now, what I'd like to suggest is that we donate it to charity. I've been making a few enquiries, and there is a Cheshire-based charity that provides help for single mothers. If we deed the house to the charity then they can either use it to provide accommodation or sell it and use the money in other ways. What do you think?'

'I think it's an excellent idea.'

'I agree.'

'So that's decided, then.'

'There might be one small problem,' Ruby

warned. 'Since Ilios cleared the mortgage, I rather suspect that Sander and Raphael will want to match his donation.'

Once again all three of them looked towards their husbands, exchanging smiles when the men looked back.

Three such male and strong men—strong enough to admit that they had been conquered by love and to show openly just how much that love meant to them.

'We are so very lucky,' Ruby announced, knowing that she was speaking for her sisters as well as for herself.

Sander, who had detached himself from Ilios and Raphael and was on his way towards them, overheard her, and stopped to tell her firmly, 'No, it is we who are the lucky ones. Lucky and blessed by the gods and by fate to have won the love of three such true Graces.'

MILLS & BOON PUBLISH EIGHT LARGE PRINT TITLES A MONTH. THESE ARE THE EIGHT TITLES FOR OCTOBER 2010.

MARRIAGE: TO CLAIM HIS TWINS
Penny Jordan

THE ROYAL BABY REVELATION
Sharon Kendrick

UNDER THE SPANIARD'S LOCK AND KEY
Kim Lawrence

SWEET SURRENDER WITH THE MILLIONAIRE
Helen Brooks

MIRACLE FOR THE GIRL NEXT DOOR
Rebecca Winters

MOTHER OF THE BRIDE
Caroline Anderson

WHAT'S A HOUSEKEEPER TO DO?
Jennie Adams

TIPPING THE WAITRESS WITH DIAMONDS
Nina Harrington

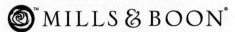

MILLS & BOON PUBLISH EIGHT LARGE PRINT TITLES A MONTH. THESE ARE THE EIGHT TITLES FOR NOVEMBER 2010.

A NIGHT, A SECRET...A CHILD
Miranda Lee

HIS UNTAMED INNOCENT
Sara Craven

THE GREEK'S PREGNANT LOVER
Lucy Monroe

THE MÉLENDEZ FORGOTTEN MARRIAGE
Melanie Milburne

AUSTRALIA'S MOST ELIGIBLE BACHELOR
Margaret Way

THE BRIDESMAID'S SECRET
Fiona Harper

CINDERELLA: HIRED BY THE PRINCE
Marion Lennox

THE SHEIKH'S DESTINY
Melissa James